QUEEN OF THE ROCKIES

QUEEN OF THE ROCKIES SERIES-BOOK 1

ANGELA BREIDENBACH

God bless!

Angie

God bless!

Onyi

CONTENTS

QUEEN OF THE ROCKIES

QUEEN OF THE ROCKIES SERIES — BOOK 1

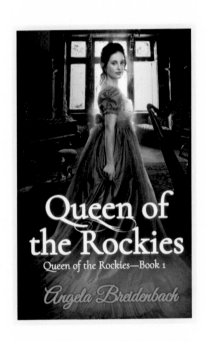

ACKNOWLEDGMENTS

Thank you to friends and family that sacrificed time during some huge events so this book could come to fruition. You are so loved! I also want to thank the Missoula Public Library for the extensive Montana history collection they keep that allows such amazing historical and genealogical discovery.

A special thank you to my friend, Valerie Comer, for brainstorming and being part of the original idea for Snowflake Tiara where we published two books together as one, mine—The Debutante Queen, and hers—More Than A Tiara. I have treasured memories of our research and promotion trips, our first book, and our friendship.

NOTE TO READERS

I'm excited to share with you a story that celebrates not only Montana's statehood, but also the capitol city, Helena! The people that built this amazing state come from varying backgrounds that include immigrants from countries like Ireland, China, Japan, Germany, Scotland, Sweden, and so many more…

But it wasn't just the adults that pioneered and persevered. Children from all over the country swarmed the streets of these fledgling cities. Some as abandoned orphans dropped at the last stop on the famous Orphan Train. Some orphaned due to disease, mining accidents, or severe weather disasters. And some, well, no one rightly knows. But my genealogist heart had to dig into Montana's history and some of the colorful, lively people that helped form this amazing state to find out more. Many names in this book are straight from Montana's history. As a professional genealogist, I felt it was important to share them for the sake of families that might be searching out their ancestors and discover a little more than they could on their own.

If you find your ancestor in these pages, please drop me a note via AngelaBreidenbach.com on my contact page. I might know more than I wrote, as is often the case. Writers can't use everything we've uncovered through research or we'd bog down the story being told.

In this story, one woman who thought she was a misfit leads social change. One person who thought she didn't matter became the unexpected example. Scared, unsure of what to do our heroine chooses to do the right thing. People can feel like a misfit regardless of financial or social status. My experience and research has shown that it's exactly those "misfits" that change the world. Personally, I embrace my "misfit" self now. I hope you will, too, if you feel like you don't quite fit the normal way of being. You're not necessarily supposed to fit in, if you're living for the purpose(s) you were uniquely made to achieve. (Who said you have only one purpose? I'm just sayin'.)

"Who knows if perhaps you were made queen for just such a time as this?"

Esther 4:14, NLT

Esther was called to cry out for her people. She was famous, beautiful, and in a position to do something great. But she didn't know she'd be put there. She was a nobody from the wrong people, according to the popular people. Have you ever felt like that? I know I have.

We hear the above verse often. But how often do we realize the wisdom is not only for a "special" person whose fame, money, or position grants them opportunity? Like Esther, she started out as a nobody, we are each called to a special purpose. Like Esther, we won't likely recognize the time has come until we're in the moment.

These Old Testament people are examples God uses to show each of us how to respond when we're asked to step up. None of us know what that calling will look like. For one it's saving a child, for another standing up to the crowd, and yet another could be called to care for an elder.

What struck me as I wrote Queen of the Rockies? What if I'm called to support someone else when they're facing intense opposition? Could I be the handmaid or friend asked to fast and pray? Could I be Mordecai challenging Haman, foster parent to the next queen, leader of a people group? Could I be the king holding out the scepter? One of many facing persecution? A voice crying out for justice? Who am I in God's plan? Will I willingly go where He leads even when I don't understand the plan?

Lord, I will go where you send me because You placed me in such a place at such a time for just this purpose—even if I'm scared, confused, or don't think I'm the right one.

Angela Breidenbach

PS Keep reading through for a bonus travel guide article about visiting Helena, MT and a peek at the next book in the series, *Song of the Rockies*.

CHAPTER 1

Queen of the Rockies

Therefore all things whatsoever ye would that men should do to you, do ye even so to them: for this is the law and the prophets. Matthew 7: 12, KJV

*H*elena, Montana Territory
November 7, 1889

STOP THAT!" Calista Blythe wrestled her skirts free from the insistent waif. "What are you doing?" She twisted around in a circle as she collapsed the umbrella, dodging packages as they tumbled. Calista waited for her carriage to circle back down Main Street, the newly erected Power Building's massive stone walls seemed a good idea to keep her out of the sharp wind. But

Calista hadn't counted on a street urchin to mug her. They were getting too brazen — and desperate —with winter descending on Montana. What could she do about dozens of orphans dumped off of trains? Something had to be done for the abandoned children no one adopted when they reached the last stop on the Orphan Train route. No one did. Calista's heart squeezed a little.

The child twisted her hands into Calista's blue velvet coat and held on like a bedraggled kitten clawed into a tree trunk. "Please miss, don't let 'im whip me no more." The little girl whimpered in a heavy Irish brogue as tears ran muddy rivers on her reddened cheeks, and she trembled in the cold.

"Who?" Calista craned to see around the corner of the grayish pink battered stone of the business building that served Helena, Montana's Last Chance Gulch. She caught sight of Albert Shanahan's handsome, stunned face as he endured confrontation with an angry manservant. The thin switch whistled through the air and slapped against the butler's gloved palm.

Calista's body rattled with an involuntary shudder. "Oh my!" Calista ducked back before she drew attention as the manservant entered a nearby shop. Had the little bumpkin been whacked with that weapon? "Why are you in trouble?"

A nearby door rattled against the wind. The manservant's growling voice carried on the sharp, cold wind from a shop doorway. "If you see the little chit, you'll let me know immediately. Yes? She's been nothing but trouble since Chicago Joe purchased her indenture. Stupid Irish whelp." The bell jangled as wind mixed with a light snow forced the door closed behind him. Then his footsteps pounded on the walkway coming close.

The dirty little girl pressed against rough-cut stones of the enormous Power Block building. She hunkered down and whispered, "Please—" Her petite frame seemed like an ant against the massive structure housing multiple businesses. Helena, a city blooming with intricate pink and gray stone and brick architecture on Main Street, sprouted buildings that encompassed an entire block.

Calista pushed backward, adjusting her skirts until the child disappeared into the frills and ruffles of her blue velvet coat and day dress. From the looks of her, the material would add warmth to the quivering little body. Calista opened her reticule and pretended to search inside as the man stomped to the arced stairway.

He took a long look between the tall buildings.

She peeked between lowered lashes. Adjusting the strings and juggling the velvet purse into her overloaded basket, Calista worked to appear as one of the flustered many preparing for the festivities the next day when the president would sign Montana into the union as the 41st state.

Calista waited a few minutes before glancing after the black-suited manservant. Orphans, too long ignored and neglected, needed safety and schooling. This little one seemed to have a home, though not a safe one. Calista's heart constricted. Why did people treat other people this way?

She couldn't loiter on a busy street concealing an indentured servant all day. What if Mr. Shanahan saw her unexpected secret? What would she do with the little urchin then? Return her for a beating? Calista closed her eyes. Not if it was within her ability to stop it!

"Is he gone?" The little one poked her head around Calista's skirts, sniffled, and ran her nose along a grubby sleeve.

"I think so." She bent to meet the child's eye-level. The girl was so small and poorly dressed for the weather in a calf-length wool work smock. A light snow melted into spattering rain. The clouds broke for an occasional glimpse of sunshine, but not enough to dry the wet, muddy gulch or warm the blue-lipped child. Not enough to keep anyone from a chill without proper protection. Calista's heart squeezed. "Oh child! Where are your shoes? Don't you have a shawl or coat?"

The girl's woolen stockings stank from the wet ground. "No, miss. I didna have time for 'em." Her Irish trill beautiful in contrast to the horror of her situation.

"You sound lovely, like a little meadowlark." Calista lifted the heavy velvet coatskirt and pulled the little girl against her warmth. As she wrapped the tiny shoulders, she couldn't feel more than skin and bones. "What's your name?" Warm soup and dry clothing would help, but she still needed to know why the child ran in fear. Had she done something terrible? Could some intervention help?

"I be Lea Murphy, miss." The heart-shaped pixie face looked up through strands of mussed brownish hair.

"Lea Murphy." Calista smiled. "How pretty your name is, and so are you under that grime."

Lea shivered and stared at her soaked feet, little toes crossing and rubbing. "I don't want to be pretty, miss."

What an unusual response. "Well, Lea, maybe you can tell me a little more about your situation."

She shook her head, but pressed closer in a shivered spasm.

"Here comes my driver. If you'll tell me why you think you're in such trouble, I'll see what I can do to help. Would you like a bowl of soup to warm up? Then we can get you home safe."

Lea's tears started again, and she sniffled. "I ca—," she hiccupped. "I canna — go home." She let out a wail that could bring back the man with the switch. As soon as the sound leapt from her throat, Lea clamped a dirty hand across her mouth.

Calista's stomach plummeted. What if that horrible man heard? She moved onto the sidewalk and glanced in both directions as if she wondered where the sound originated. He must have gone into another shop. Only the two men, Mr. Shanahan and Mr. T. C. Power, with backs to the sudden gust, remained near the bank's front steps. They didn't seem to hear anything above the wind.

Thank you, Lord. A smile lit her face as she signaled to the

Blythe family driver. The sun blinked behind a cloud. "Thank you, again, Lord. Your timing is perfect."

Lea looked up at the sky. "I dinna t'ink he much listens, miss."

Calista hugged her and smiled. "I think he just did."

But Lea didn't return the smile.

The carriage splashed through a puddle and pulled to a stop alongside the nearest hitching post. Calista's driver swung down and stopped short at the sight of his mistress' skirt bundle. "Miss Blythe?"

In that moment, Calista followed the nudge in her spirit. "We have a surprise guest for lunch, Charles. Please tuck a blanket around her and pull the curtains. She's quite cold."

"A lost one, huh?" The driver spun a blanket around Lea. Not a bit of the mite could be seen, but a small sigh floated back to Calista. Charles tucked the blanket end under and slid a warmed brick beneath her feet.

A tiny head poked out of the bundle from the corner of the carriage. She could be any little girl headed home for an afternoon nap. Except for the tangled hair and dirty cheeks.

Calista climbed in beside Lea and tossed a furry robe across them both. "Home, please." What would her parents do when she brought home not only a child, but one that appeared to live in the gulch gutters?

The coach pulled away from the bank building where Mr. Shanahan's impassioned speech held Mr. T. C. Power captivated. Maybe the conversation kept them from noticing anything — unusual. Any other day Calista would love to catch Mr. Shanahan's eye. Many of the city's debutantes thought him quite extraordinary husband material with his congenial personality, good looks, and excellent social connections. But today...

He looked up as the carriage passed. Mr. Shanahan's blue eyes warmed her like a hot springs soak at the new natatorium as he smiled and tipped his top hat.

Calista's mouth went dry. Could he read her nervousness? She smiled with a nodded recognition and slipped the window cover in place — and waited, heart thumping hard as cattle running across hard ground. No shout. No chaos in the streets. Calista heaved a sigh as she sent up a prayer of thanks the men hadn't realized Miss Calista Blythe had just stolen someone's child!

CHAPTER 2

*A*lbert Shanahan, you're tetched!"

"In what way, Mr. Power?" Albert rubbed his chin. "This is the city of Helena's silver anniversary. Twenty-five hard-working years and we're finally due to become a state any day, too." He swung a hand out encompassing the city street. "We won the vote to be the state capitol from Anaconda. How can we continue into the future without establishing tourism and commerce in a nationally recognized manner as we join the States?"

"But a pageant? Who will even agree to compete?" The wealthy Mr. Power shook his head. "And to what end?"

"We have an abundance of debutantes this year. Society loves parties and galas. But we struggle with winter business. What happens when the mines run out?" Albert pointed to the brick and granite buildings of Last Chance Gulch. "Combine it with a once in a lifetime opportunity to be the very first queen of the city — it's bound to succeed. A lovely girl promotes Helena as modern and elegant as any in America or Europe. She's hailed as the most beautiful girl in Montana for a year, not just of our Queen City of the Rockies. Our gold mining isn't going to last forever. Just think of all the strikes that petered out in California,

Colorado, and elsewhere. Then what? Do we let Helena become a ghost town, too?"

"Excuse me, sirs," a tall manservant interrupted. "My apologies, but have you noticed a runaway child?" The man's eyes scanned the street. "I'm chasing down an errant girl, about six, and a bit small for her age. She's managed to distress my mistress."

"Not I." Albert caught a swirl of skirts around the corner by the bank stairs.

"Nor I. Good luck in your quest. It's a bit nippy out for a little one today."

"Yes, yes." The man scowled. "Thank you for your time, gentlemen. She's due a good switching, that girl!" His switch slapped into a black-gloved palm.

Poor kid was in for a sore behind soon. Albert's peripheral vision caught a blur of blue as the woman dashed backward.

The manservant stalked up the block checking in each storefront.

Albert's tall black hat blew off backward into the street. He turned to snag it off the ground before the trolley ran it over. The sky spit a bit, but the gusting breeze couldn't quite let go of its mercurial temperament.

The trolley's bell clanged a warning. Albert jumped from the puddled road near the rail to the sidewalk. The lovely figure of the woman in the velvet dress coat trimmed in white fur faced away from him by the side of Mr. Power's building. Albert's eyes widened. Miss Blythe?

He'd only crossed paths with her a few times since she'd come back from the etiquette and finishing school last spring. But each time left Albert hoping for another. The freshly built Tomah Inn kept his days hopping. He expected to have it fully staffed, but that wouldn't be possible until the establishment had a successful winter income — or a strong event like a pageant. He didn't regret building well, but now the Tomah Inn simply must earn its income.

He glanced again, hoping not to be conspicuous, but couldn't tell from behind. She seemed to be speaking to someone blocked from his view.

Mr. Power waited, watching him with a quizzical expression.

Albert laughed. "See there? We're so modern our trolleys run on schedule — sometimes."

"Only when the companies aren't at odds." The other man's gaze followed the trolley down the rail headed to the new Broadwater Hotel and Natatorium advertised on its every available surface. "Wouldn't it be triumphant if our debutantes managed to put an end to the trolley territorial battles? One would think with the intelligence it takes for modern invention to move us from horse-drawn to steam and electric trolleys, men would have the intelligence to get along." T. C. Power looked back at his young friend and laughed. "She may be a possible solution, your tourism queen. A pretty face always softens a man's heart if that little gal over there is any example." He sent a pointed glance in the direction Albert had been staring. "Perhaps you're onto something."

Albert dusted off his hat, "I'm a bit lost. How would a winter pageant solve the trolley system problem? Mr. Broadwater and Mr. Hauser argue a good bit more over the railroads and banks they own. The trolley system, or rather the citizens of Helena trying to get to work on time, seem merely another victim of their disagreements."

"Why not put these battling businessmen to work for you!" The enthusiasm roared out of him. "I dare say if a true visionary really wanted to move our little city into the next century, then he'd use his idea to build trusted relationships with our retailers, transportation, and tourism." He grinned and slapped Albert on the back. "Yes, I do think you're onto something, young man."

Mystified, Albert looked down the trolley track and back at his older friend. "How exactly could I do that, sir?"

"Won't you need judges?"

As the clouds broke above, the light brought the brilliance

home. "Of course! Use the competition to put businessmen in an arena with a common cause so they're forced to work together. They lay down trivial grudges, focus on the future, and we'll no longer be viewed as the wilds of the west." Albert marveled at the capitalist's foresight. "You're saying ask both Broadwater and Hauser to be judges?"

"Success in business, my boy, is about timing and relationships." He tapped his temple. "But it's also about ingenuity. You might be in the midst of all three." Mr. Power pursed his lips. "Tell me more."

"Within a few days we become a state. By Christmas the entire nation will know of Helena's elegance." More ideas clamored as if the trolley bell clapped in his head. "I'll begin building a network of business support. The debutantes will come from all over the state, wherever the trains run. My inn can be the pageant headquarters." Not far away, at the edge of the fast-growing mansion district, the Tomah Inn offered quick access to downtown and walking distance for society strollers to visit friends.

"If the meetings are held at a more neutral location, the other overnight establishments might feel less competitive."

Always appreciative of his mentor's wisdom, Albert agreed. "True. Could we meet in one of your larger offices?"

"I'd be happy to help." Mr. Power flipped out his pocket watch. "Anything that builds business is a boon."

"We'll hold events at various venues to attract attention not only to businesses that fare well in winter, but also to show the popularity and cooperation of Helena's businesses."

"Now you're talking, my boy, now you're talking." Mr. Power held out a hand. "I believe you're turning out to be a shrewd entrepreneur. Why, next you'll be joining me in the Montana Club, my boy. You'll be a millionaire yet with that head on your shoulders. We all prosper when we work together."

Albert took his hand in a firm grip. "Even Anaconda has a new paper. We'll get in all the society columns. Surely the bigger cities will see the newsworthiness as well." This pageant was no longer the smallish, original idea to bring tourism to one city year round. But blossomed into a grand opportunity to share Helena society, and the new state of Montana, to the world. If he could build trust in the city as a tourist destination, Helena could survive even when the gold mines dried up. But as the capitol, she'd represent the entire state — and so would his queen.

"Well then, young Albert, I imagine you're off to drum up participants in this new endeavor. What will you call it?"

"Yes, sir." Albert smiled. "The Snowflake Pageant has a nice ring to it for a winter extravaganza. I thank you for allowing me to detain you."

"Not at all, not at all. It may be that you'll find one of those debutantes for your own, perhaps? I hear tell your dear mama believes it's high time." Mr. Power laughed at his own words.

"Yes, she's made it plainly and, I fear, publicly known she has an eligible bachelor for a son." Albert cocked his head to see if the woman in blue still stood near the building corner. "I believe I'm uniquely well acquainted with a large majority of eligible young ladies." He gave a self-deprecating laugh. But one young lady drew his interest time and again.

Mr. Power turned and traced Albert's line of sight. "Somehow I don't think you're thinking of just any debutante right now."

Albert turned away with a shrug. Was it that apparent?

A carriage drew up to the curbside. The driver spoke to Miss Blythe, grabbed a blanket, tucked it around something behind the lady, and stuffed it inside the carriage. A child? Albert shook his head. She must have purchased a garden statue. Trains brought so many niceties now. But then how did she get it to the side of the Power Building? She'd been speaking to someone. A delivery to her pick up point?

Miss Blythe looked both ways, up and down Main Street, before entering the carriage.

Albert watched the horses pull past and scanned the window for a glimpse of the girl he'd first noticed a few summers before he'd been sent to school in Denver. With her hand on the curtain, Miss Blythe's eyes widened but she smiled a greeting. Lovelier now, his opportunity would be short before someone snatched her away.

Mr. Power added with a wink, "I think you do have a certain lady in mind, Albert, lad. I think you do."

Albert cleared his throat. "Excuse me?" He blinked and brought his mind back to matters of importance. What Miss Blythe purchased today was none of his concern, but the future of Helena's tourism might make a fledgling businessman into husband material — and then perhaps knowing what Miss Blythe purchased in the future would matter to a husband.

Mr. Power stretched a hand out, grinning. "That particular debutante would set them all in a flurry. Good luck to you, lad." They shook. "On all counts." With a tip of his hat, he walked up the stairs and into the bank.

He'd need it — on all counts. Albert could see the beginning of Helena's legitimacy in the eyes of the nation. Though a pretty brunette woman in blue velvet vied for first place against the vision for Albert's attention. How could he get further acquainted with the lovely Miss Calista Blythe unless her parents recognized his potential? Would they consider an affluent innkeeper for a son-in-law? Especially among the overly available wealthy male choices?

Albert had only one choice. Become wealthy enough his manner of income didn't matter in this nouveau riche society, only that he could support a wife to her parents' expectations. Not an easy task with over fifty millionaires in Helena already and more joining their ranks from gold strikes weekly.

CHAPTER 3

*L*ea?" Calista popped her head around the carriage door. Her eyes widened at the emptiness. Gone? Even the thick fur blanket Calista had left tucked around the little one wasn't inside. "Lea? Come now, I've prepared a spot for you to rest. Aren't you hungry?"

Where in the world could a little girl go in the space of five minutes? Especially one with a hungry tummy and no shoes!

Calista searched the carriage house, horse stalls, and finally under the carriage. Nothing. The little girl wouldn't speak on the ride home. Now she disappeared. Well, two could play at this game. She took one more look around the carriage house, and then went to the kitchen. Lea would have to come out sooner or later — and she'd be ravenous.

"Mrs. Brown, would you kindly make a hearty snack plate for me? I'm afraid I didn't have much time for a reasonable lunch."

"I'd be happy to, Miss Calista." More than a servant, she smiled as if she knew a secret. A moment later Mrs. Brown placed a plate full of biscuits with butter and jam, cheese, and ham in Calista's hands. "Just a few minutes and I'll have a cup of warm milk."

"But—"

Mrs. Brown held up her hand. "You'll have enough explaining to do with your parents. Go find whatever waif you've brought on home this time. I'd consider keeping it to sparrows and kittens, though. Your mama may not take well to strangers in the house. I certainly hope it's not a criminal you've hidden in the carriage house."

Calista looked up from the piled food. "Oh no!"

"Well, best you keep Charles close by and be safe." She pulled out the dishcloth and wiped crumbs from the cutting board.

"Mrs. Brown, please don't say anything until I can speak with my parents. I'm trying to help a little girl who seemed to be in quite a quandary."

Mrs. Brown stopped halfway to the dustbin. "A little girl?" She dropped the crumbs right onto the floor. "Well go get her on into the warm house. My goodness, a little girl … I'll get a warm bath upstairs …" Mrs. Brown's words trailed off as she bustled out of the kitchen.

Calista swung back out the door to tempt little Lea inside.

"No, no, no!" Captain Blythe flourished a hand through the air, cutting like a saber. "What in the world made you step into a legal mire like that? Snatching a child off the streets — where is her mother?"

"Papa, I don't know yet." Calista clasped her hands. "I had to coax her out of the hay with a plate of food. The little mite barely trusted me enough to come into the kitchen."

"Where is she now, dear?" Eloise Blythe leaned forward. "Your father is right. He knows these things."

"Mama, she fell asleep on her plate. I couldn't very well toss her back in the barn, now could I?" Her stomach clenched at the vivid picture Lea presented clambering out of the hay for ham and biscuits. The warmed milk lulled the tyke to sleep after her teeth stopped chattering.

"Calista, your mother asked you a question." His stern countenance brooked no further avoidance.

Calista took a deep breath, let it out, and answered. "I tucked her into a cot in my room."

"So I am to understand that we are, at this very moment, harboring a runaway child who is legally under an indenture contract?" His bushy brows rammed into one another.

"A starving, cold, lost little soul. Papa, you should see her. If she has a mother, which I'm not certain she does, then it's possible her mama isn't capable of feeding or clothing or even educating Lea."

"Ah, Lea. You've already formed an attachment like the little creatures you've brought home since childhood." Captain Blythe struck a match to his pipe. "She has to go back to her mother and the owner of her indenture, or the authorities, immediately."

Calista leapt from her chair in the salon, "But Papa —"

"Daughter, I'm both a lawyer and an outdoorsman. When you pluck a chick from its nest, you either become responsible for its life when the mother rejects it or you find a way to release it back to nature."

"But Papa, Lea isn't a wild creature. She's a child!"

"And you've already become attached to someone not your concern as you did with the baby duck, the rabbit, and a host of other wild animals. There are legal ramifications when it comes to a human. You can't simply collect a child like you would a — puppy. If there's no mother and she proves not to be indentured, then an orphan home is the proper place. She'll be well cared for in the most appropriate circumstance."

"But Papa!" Calista turned to her mother and grasped her lacey wrist. "Mama, can't you make him see Lea needs me?"

"She does not need a young single girl with no funds of her own. Just how would you care for her?"

"I thought you'd help me. It's one little girl, Papa."

"What about the rest of them out there? We can't take them all in. If we start with one, where does it end? No, there's a social problem that needs solving here and we cannot be an orphan farm because we're the last stop on the orphan train route. We'd crumble under the sheer volume. Solve the social problem and you'll help the little girl, and all the children like her. Join your mother's cause. That's the only way."

"Mama, please?"

Eloise clamped her lips closed and shook her head. Then her face softened. "Come help me get women a vote. Then we can make a real change in the lives of all these street children. Would you help one child or one hundred?"

"Mama, even the Lord went after one out of ninety-nine."

"But unless it's legal, we cannot be a part of it. At this moment, Calista, you don't even know she's truly an orphan, do you? And that makes you — what is it, dear?" She turned to her husband.

"You're either a kidnapper or you're interfering in a legality without enough information to be acting in the best interest of the child. Either way, return her to where she belongs this instant."

"Mama, Papa …"

"Not another word, Calista!" Her father's face darkened and his voice lowered. "Do the right thing."

How is this not the right thing? Out of the corner of her eye, Calista caught a glimpse of a brown dress. No! Did she hear this exchange?

A door slammed and echoed through the kitchen.

"Oh no!" Calista lifted her skirt and chased after Lea.

CHAPTER 4

*E*xcuse me, sir." Calista approached the stern man, dressed identically to the day prior in a pristine black butler's suit. Swallowing back her worries, she had to know Lea survived the night. "Weren't you the fellow looking for the child yesterday?" The mid-morning sun peeked precariously in between clouds as if it could be snuffed out like a candle at any moment.

"Yes, Jasper Chambers, miss. Did you find her?"

"No, I —" Calista hadn't thought further than inquiring. "I simply hoped you had. It's quite cold out for a child to be lost on the streets."

"She isn't lost, miss. She ran away from her responsibilities."

"A small child? What responsibilities could she possibly have?"

"She owes Chicago Joe money."

"For what? Chicago Joe runs — oh! But you described a very little girl." Calista's voice rose and dripped disapproval.

"Look, miss, Chicago Joe paid for the mother to come all the way from the east on the train. She done brought the brat with her. Then they both arrived sick."

Calista's hand clutched the buttons on her brocade coat. "Sick? The little girl is sick?"

"No, her mother died, but the scamp recovered. Now she must work off the transport and doctor bills for both of them according to the indenture agreement."

"You can't be serious!" Calista stamped a foot. "Her mother is … dead. Wouldn't the contract have been with her mother?"

He waved a document at her. "Miss, it's all legal and such. The indenture passes to the child."

Did he have to carry the certificate around flapping it in people's faces? "How exactly do you expect a child to pay off bills for a dead mother?"

"Miss, she's an indentured servant. That's the way it works. I'm checking if some do-gooder took her in and this is my proof of ownership." The wind whipped the paper like a sheet on a laundry line. The snapping threatened to tear it from his hand. Mr. Chambers slipped it in an inside pocket near his chest. "It's not your trouble."

As if that washed away all humanity! "Well, I'll pay it then. A little girl like that shouldn't be saddled with bills. How much is it?"

"One hundred and two dollars. And that doesn't cover room and board or lost income."

Calista gasped. "That much?" How in the world would Lea ever be free? "What do you expect her to do to pay off that ransom?" Even her monthly allowance wouldn't add up to enough for months.

"I told you it wasn't your trouble." The man narrowed his eyes and leaned in close to Calista's face. "Unless you know something?"

Calista took a step backward. Not a thing in the world would make her hand over Lea now. She squared her shoulders and repeated her thoughts out loud. "No, not a thing."

He searched her face, gave a curt nod, and then strode away scouting the streets.

Would God consider that a sin of omission? Telling the truth to the wrong person had to be wrong—right? Especially if it meant a child would be raised slaving in a bawdy house. Regardless, Calista committed in her heart to hold Lea's well-being higher than the law. Wasn't that the right thing to do…somehow?

Calista watched his back, coattails violently thrashing, wishing she could run after him and pay the funds. But with ten dollars to finish her daily shopping and buy a few presents for Christmas, that was only a small percentage of the need. If only a tithe would solve it. What could she do? Her parents would never support purchasing Lea's indenture. They'd made it clear they believed in the legal system as a solution.

Besides, Lea disappeared right out of the Blythe home. Exposed to the cold, how could Lea have survived the freezing night? If found, could Calista prevail on someone gentler than Lea's current supposed indentured position to purchase her? Who would need a small girl — possibly in a kitchen? Someone kind enough to be sure Lea received food, clothing, and an education?

A sponsor. She'd find an orphan sponsor.

"Miss Blythe." Albert Shanahan tipped his hat as he smiled into Calista's eyes. "Are you here to attend the swearing in?"

"Why Mr. Shanahan, what a pleasure." She dipped her head, and a tight brown curl escaped a pin in the strong, frigid breeze. "Swearing in?" Tucking the curl back under the wide, cocoa brown brim of her hat turned into a battle between gloved fingers and loose pins. A pin slipped into the glove's seam stitches, pulling more stylish curls from the elaborate coiffure when she tugged away. Calista reddened.

Mr. Shanahan turned toward the street, as if to give her a moment to control the mayhem the wind created. "We're finally a state. The great state of Montana! The wire came a short time ago and the first governor will take his oath shortly. The papers won't carry it for a day or two." His eyes held hers. "But you're here in time to be part of an historic occasion."

A flutter tickled up from Calista's belly. She dropped her gaze and concentrated on the errant coif. There. Calista patted her hat and hair into a semblance of order, if minus a few pins that clattered to the ground. She smoothed the matching cocoa coat skirt and gown against the onslaught of the sharp breeze. "How exciting! Papa will be there, I'm sure." Maybe, with enough people celebrating, spirits would be high. Surely someone would be in a grand mood and primed for generosity toward a little girl. The coming parties would mean a need for more help, even the most basic like peeling potatoes or helping brush down guests' horses. "It's been so long in coming, I can hardly believe it's true."

"I'd be proud to escort you to the event so you may hear the auspicious words yourself." He offered an elbow and looked expectant.

A heavy gust blew the feathers from her hat backward, pulling the mass of curls into a frenzy further twisting and tangling hair, hat, and pins. "Oh!" Calista squeaked. She grabbed at the hat releasing more of her maple brown hair as pins flew to the sidewalk and into the hard packed dirt road. Yet the hat hung hackled to a tousle of tresses against her ear — until it flapped in a new flurry slapping against Calista's face, relentless as if a tree refused to release fall foliage.

Mr. Shanahan's lips twitched. "May I assist?" He pulled off his own gloves and snatched her hat as another draught ripped it loose from the riot of long strands unraveling like a spool of yarn into his hands.

Calista covered her face, but winced at Mr. Shanahan's erupting laughter. Why hadn't she covered her ears instead? Who would take her seriously about the plight of an orphan girl when she looked like one herself?

✳

ALBERT TUCKED Miss Blythe's hat under his arm. Taking both her hands, he drew them away from her adorable face. A woman never looked so beautiful to him. Blue eyes opened like a new cornflowers sending a chinook right through his soul. The arctic blast against his back couldn't compete with the spring inside his heart. He watched her intently, replaying the feel of her soft hair against his palms.

Then she trembled. Dew laced her lashes until droplets trickled from the corner of one lovely oval eye. "Thank you for your — " Miss Blythe cleared her throat and tipped her head away. "I'll ... I'll be on my way."

"I'm terribly sorry. I meant no disrespect. Your hat played quite the femme fatale." He smiled and proffered the villainous millenary marvel. T.C. Power was right. The lovely Miss Blythe, and her mass of brown ringlets, would be the perfect contestant. So graceful and contained in embarrassing circumstances. She'd be the perfect role model. Every debutante in town would follow her lead, and enter the pageant, as they already did in fashion. One nod for or against the bonnet, why hats like these would be outlawed in society by tomorrow.

Pushing down his desire to take her in his arms, he swallowed. What would convince Miss Calista Blythe to compete for Miss Snowflake? But then he couldn't ask to court her for another year.

A smile crept up on her as if the sun spread its arms in the sky to banish the storm. "Thank you. A femme fatale?"

"Yes, quite the wicked attack on an innocent bystander. Wouldn't you say? Shall I call the authorities?" But she'd be working closely with him. He could be patient as they learned more about one another over the course of a year. Couldn't he? The rules would keep other men away as he captured her heart. Miss Blythe's rich giggle sang through his blood until he stood drenched in a waterfall of her laughter.

"Miss Blythe, might I ask you to consider entering the Miss Snowflake pageant?" He fished into his breast pocket and produced a small application card made up to look like an invitation.

"A pageant?"

"With your entry, we're sure to have a successful event. Would you consider it?"

"Whatever is it for, Mr. Shanahan? I'm sure my father wouldn't approve of me parading in public like a —"

"Oh no, Miss Blythe, no! This is a celebration of both our statehood and to show the refinement of Montana society. We must succeed into the next century in business and tourism. Miss Snowflake will be our new tourism queen. A representative of Montana's grace and elegance. Her duties will be to help Helena, and Montana, become recognized as Queen of the Rockies to the rest of the world. Our businesses and economy depend on drawing tourists year round."

Miss Blythe smiled and took the card.

Politeness? An effort to close the conversation? Or could she possibly be considering his request?

Then she said, "It's a lovely idea, thank you. Any girl would be honored to play such a part in our future. But I don't think that girl is me."

"But would you —"

She shook her head and laid a halting hand on his arm. "I really must be going. I've, well, I've lost something that must be found."

"I'll help you search. Tell me, what is it? Something from your excursion yesterday?"

"My what?" Her eyes opened wide as her face turned white.

Albert stepped backward. "Again, I apologize for my forwardness. You were here yesterday. Your driver, he carried something to the carriage. Perhaps you lost something then?"

A shutter snapped in her eyes. "No. It was after that, thank you."

"Where did you go? Perhaps —"

Miss Blythe held out a hand. "No, no thank you." The wind

ruffled the dark sable fur around her cuffs and collar framing her face like a locket.

What had he done? "Miss Blythe, I only seek to help." His scarf lifted and smacked into his face as if part of a conspiracy to hold him back a few paces, or put him in his place.

The Blythe carriage driver, Charles, appeared around the corner. She flagged him to a stop and nearly beat him to opening the carriage door.

Charles glanced both ways, not at the ground, as he helped Miss Blythe inside the carriage. "Anything, Miss?"

Why hadn't her man looked toward the ground where a lost object might be found?

"No, Charles. We must keep searching. I'm most concerned." With a stiff glance over her shoulder, the pretty young lady nodded. "Good morning, Mr. Shanahan."

He gave a courteous half bow. "Miss Blythe."

As they pulled away, ahead of an oncoming trolley steaming up the track, the tail of a wooly rug flapped from the lid of the rear boot.

Albert pulled the furry brown hat from under his arm. A smile spread across his lips. A gentleman ought to return a lady's expensive hat. That gallantry might win her over. At least it'd win him a little bit of time.

"Charles, let's search the entire property once again. She can't have gotten far on those tiny legs. She might even be — " Calista's gloved hand flew to stop the words from escaping. No, Lea had to be in the hay or in the storage cellar or somewhere hiding safely.

"We'll find her." Charles lifted a hand to help her down the carriage step.

"Not a word to anyone. I can't let that horrid man take her back. Imagine forcing a tiny tot like that to work off her mother's debt, no less. Indentured or not, she can't help what happens to someone else. She had no choice in the matter."

"No, Miss Blythe. Indentured, you say?" Charles big shoulders slumped. "It ain't right. No, it ain't." His forehead crinkled as his attention diverted over Calista's head. Crow's feet creased into deep lines around the man's aging eyes. He put a finger to his lips and pointed behind Calista, toward the back of the carriage.

"What? Did you —" Calista saw the edge of the blanket too. The luggage box. The one place she hadn't thought to look. But the blanket hadn't poked out before.

"If'n a young critter were to hop around the barn, Miss Blythe, how do you suppose it might stay warm and survive?" He winked.

She raised her voice a tad to be sure Lea could hear her. "I suppose if there were a small warming stove in the footman's quarters, maybe some morsels of food laying around the creature could nibble, and enough burrowing material to keep warm — well a small critter, as you say, might just manage. Do you think, Charles?"

"A critter might learn to trust the kind folks that provided for it. Should I stoke the warming stove in the back in case a little critter sneaks into the carriage house and makes its way back to the footman's quarters, Miss Blythe? I'd hate for any small creatures to freeze in this here cold spell."

Both watched the blanket slowly pull back into the luggage box. Calista's twinkling eyes met Charles' deeply lined grin.

"Why yes, that would be a good precaution. Your quarters are warm, but I'm sure all the barn beasts would appreciate a bit of extra warmth during this cold spell." Calista motioned Charles toward the back room. "I'll ask Mrs. Brown to put some apple cider on in the kitchen. A bit of sweet, hot apple cider will do us all some good after that brisk outing."

Several horse stalls and cupboards lined the long building. The tiny door and room in the back would be large enough to fold out a cot while the compact quarters would hold heat in from a small warming stove. The child could feel hidden, warm, and protected while Calista worked out a solution to this dizzying dilemma.

Today of all days, she could get away with her plans while the rest of the household raced to town — as soon as she shared the good news Mr. Shanahan provided. Montana, a full-fledged state! Then she could work a little coaxing charm on one pint-sized, orphaned critter.

CHAPTER 5

*C*alista waited until everyone slept in the large home. Then sliding on her heaviest coat and slippers against the night chill, she crept through the dark to care for her unexpected secret before it could be discovered in the barn. Calista's heart beat a wild rhythm. Could she get away with this long enough to find a solution?

The barn door creaked open. Calista froze. She took a deep breath and searched in the dark for any signs of detection from the house. Charles had left an unlit lantern just inside the entry for her. Calista lit the wick. She moved quickly out of visibility, down the hallway, to avoid accidental discovery. Anyone might think Charles finished a bit of late night work, but Calista preferred not to challenge that assumption.

"Lea?" Calista whispered as she pushed the door to the tiny room open. Warm air rushed out and she quickly closed it to keep the warmth for the little girl. "Lea? Are you asleep yet?"

No answer. But the little one looked up through sad, red eyes in the lantern's glow. She didn't pull back or run to hide. The exhaustion should have helped her sleep hard as a rock. But Lea looked terrified.

Calista noticed the empty dishes on the bench. She'd eaten

every bite. *Thank you, God.* "Hello, honey, how did you like your supper?"

"It was good." Her lips trembled. "Thank you, miss."

Calista took a step closer. If Lea didn't run, she'd try another. "Miss?"

"You can call me Miss Calista." She said as she lowered slowly onto the end of the cot.

Lea nodded. "Miss Calista, your papa said I had to go back. You gonna send me back?"

"No, Lea, not if I can help it." A muffled mew sounded nearby. Hopefully the barn cats wouldn't bother Lea too much. Sometimes they could be over-friendly and other times their yowling fights caused a ruckus.

Lea pushed her hands into the lumpy quilt. "But then won't you get switched?" Her eyes grew as big as a full moon. "I don't want you to get switched nei-ver."

"I won't. But I am looking for a better place for you. Somewhere you'll be warm, well fed, and educated. Where there's kind people. That would be good, right?"

"This is good. I like bein' a barn critter." She nodded with the wisdom of a child and oddly patted the quilt between her feet. "You're nice and the am-i-nals like me."

"Animals." Calista corrected and smiled. Oh if only she could keep this adorable little pixie. "So you heard Charles and I?"

She nodded and hugged her knees up under the pile of quilts Calista had scrounged from the attic.

Another mew sounded very close — almost as if … a little ball under the blankets moved. Calista eyed the lump but decided to let it be. "Lea, what happened to your mommy? Can you tell me?"

"She coughed till she died," Lea whispered. "She couldn't breef no more." Tears dripped down her cheeks. "I miss my mama." She sniffled, cried harder, and rubbed her wrist across a tiny red nose. A tick jerked Lea's chin through the crying jag.

Calista felt hot tears well up in her eyes, too. She slid forward on the bunk and wrapped the little girl in her arms. "I'm so sorry." She began to hum a new song she'd learned last Christmas like a lullaby. It ironically seemed to fit this tiny tot. She began to rock until a loud mew protested the squishing movement and little black tufted ears popped out of the covers and struggled for freedom.

"N-o-o!" Lea cried harder. "I need him. I saved him like you saved me."

Calista caught the kitty in the corner and calmed it for Lea. He seemed weaned and friendly. A barn kitten wouldn't be a bad idea. He could keep Lea entertained while this dilemma resolved. "He's just a bit scared like you are. He's not used to all this attention. I think his mama is around here somewhere."

"Can I keep him?"

Lea's pleading brown eyes held depths of loneliness unlike anything Calista had ever known. What could she do? "I'll tell you what, if you take good care of him I'll bring breakfast for both of you in the morning. But he needs to stay a barn kitty. So you can keep him while you're here. But when I find you a new home, he'll need to stay with his mama. Can you do that?"

"Oh I will. I will!"

"Then we have a deal. I'll take care of you and you'll take care of him. But we both know this is just temporary, right? Until I find you a good home."

"Tempry. I don't know what tempry is, Miss Calista."

"Temp-o-rar-y. It means for a little while, not for always."

Lea's voice lowered with her head. "I don't wanna go." The tears started all over again, triggering deep jerking spams.

"I know, but a barn is no place to live for a long time. You need a real home — a safe one." Calista hummed the song again as she stroked the kitten's soft black fur and then sang the first verse in a hushed tone.

"What's that song?" She hiccupped for a breath. "I like it. My mama used to sing me to sleep." A little shudder rumbled through Lea's chest and shoulders as she took a deep breath.

"Shh, it's okay. You're safe." Calista smoothed back dirty blond hair. "It's called *Away in the Manger*. Another little boy named Jesus had to stay in a barn too. For a while, he had to be hidden away from an evil king to keep him safe. Would you like me to tell you that story?"

"Yes, please."

"Well it's a long one, so I'll tell it in parts. Yes?" At the little girl's nod, Calista continued, "There was a pretty lady named Mary about to have a baby. She knew an angel said this baby would be special and save all the people from their sins."

"An angel? I think Mama is an angel now. That's what a lady said. A pretty angel. But Mama said not to be pretty."

Obviously Lea needed more than just food and a safe home. She didn't seem to know much about heaven either. In her grief and fear, this wasn't the time to straighten out misguided theology. "Pretty isn't bad, honey. You're not bad for being pretty."

"That's what got her in trouble, she said. Mama said I needed to be plain and not be pretty so people don't notice me."

"Oh my," Calista couldn't help herself. "I bet your mommy was a very pretty lady who wanted you to be safe." She understood what would be expected of Lea. And it appeared Lea had some sort of understanding, too. That was not going to happen! How in the world would she protect Lea from being used like that? "I'll tell you what, let's finish this part of the story and work on tomorrow's troubles tomorrow."

Sleepy eyes blinked up from the pillow. The kitten stretched and yawned, then snuggled into the crook of Lea's shoulder and neck. Lea turned her cheek into the furry form.

"But Joseph, her new husband, and Mary had to go register to be counted. The king wanted to know how many people he had. So they had to go a long way. But when they arrived in Bethlehem, where they had to be counted, there was no room for them in any inns."

"No place to stay? But she was having a baby." Small fingers curled in and out of fluffy, black fur.

Calista shook her head. "And Mary started to have her baby. So one innkeeper offered to let them stay with his animals. But there was no place to put the baby when he was born. So Mary wrapped him in swaddling clothes and laid him in the manger."

"They really stayed in a barn like me?"

"They really did. I don't know what that barn looked like, but now you know you're not the first person to sleep in a barn."

"What'd his mama name him?"

"Jesus." Calista smiled and tapped the little girl's nose. "She named him Jesus. And he grew up to be our Lord and Savior. But that's for another night."

"I like that name. It's a good name for a baby." She turned on her side and snuggled the black kitten close. He'd already fallen into a purring sleep. One paw crossed over Lea's hand.

"All right then, it's time for all little barn creatures to get some sleep. I have to go back in the house so no one knows I'm gone. You'll be safe with Mr. Charles on the other side of this wall." There'd be no other way for the next few days. If she snuck the girl in the house, anyone could stumble on her. It'd be next to impossible to sneak Lea in and out when someone was nearly always home.

Calista would have to trust Charles to take turns and check on her small secret. "Try to be very quiet in the morning. Don't come out until either Charles or I come get you. I'll bring you some yummy breakfast. Can you and your kitten do that?" A few days, that's all it would take.

Lea looked at the kitten and back at Calista. She nodded against the pillow. Her new little friend would help her through the night. "And I know his name too. I know the perfect little barn boy name."

"Really? What do you want to name him?"

"Jesus." Lea pronounced it with a decisive nod. The kitten raised his head and wiggled closer to her warmth.

"Oh, he's just a kitten, honey. I don't know if that's very respectful. Our Savior's name is Jesus."

Tears started to trickle again. "Don't you think Jesus cares about kittens?"

"Of course he cares, honey. He cares about all his creatures, even kittens — even you and me." Calista cupped Lea's cheek. "If you think Jesus is the right name for this little fellow, then it is." She pecked Lea's forehead and scratched the kitten's ear. Then tucked the blankets up around them.

Calista left the doused lantern inside the barn door and snuck back into the house with silent prayers pounding through her heart. Of course it had to be raining. But at least it wasn't snow that'd show her footprints. She slid soaked slippers behind the bench by the stove to dry.

Oh Lord, I hope you really don't mind a kitten named after you. Snuggle Lea as close as she's snuggling that little kitten. Could you be as real to her please? Help me to find her the perfect family. I can't do this alone, but she can't either. A stair creaked and Calista froze. *You're listening, right, Lord?*

THE LAMPLIGHT on Albert's desk glared on the plain black and white truth. Mirielle Sheehan, Alma Goss, and Wanda Wharburton. Three girls registered. Only three. He needed more like thirty to pull off an extravaganza meant to capture national headlines. Not to mention the need for numbers to cover the one hundred dollar cash prize and the tiara he'd ordered. Something to cause papers back East to notice the gentility and beauty of the newest state and influence tourism. But without an accepting nod from Helena's societal cream, Miss Snowflake would melt into a puddle of failure — and so would the Tomah Inn without winter business.

Rain drizzled down the windowpane. Scratching his head, Albert ran through a list of ideas. He discarded all but two. Visit Miss Calista Blythe and convince her to enter the pageant — and then make sure every other debutante in Helena knew. They'd flock to the pageant. With her finishing school training at St. Benedict's, the other young ladies copied every move and every fashion style. Funny thing was, Miss Blythe didn't seem to notice. She had a humble way about her, almost naïve.

Was it wrong to use the prominence of one so well thought of to garner trust in others? Only if she disagreed … and she might dig in her heels. She'd said no once, but that was while under stress. This time he'd help her understand what was at stake. Miss Blythe couldn't refuse, could she?

CHAPTER 6

*M*r. Shanahan, sir, it's a pleasure." Charles extended his hand. "Let me help you with your horse and buggy while you go on in the house. You plannin' on stayin' long? Should I unhitch her?"

"Thank you, no." He shook the older man's hand and passed the reins. "Would you know if the ladies are in? I'm not expected."

"Why Miss Blythe sure is, sir. She was outside getting a breath of air a moment ago." Charles winked. "I'm sure it'll be a right fine visit."

"I hope so. I certainly hope so." He snagged Calista's brown hat from the bench seat.

Albert went around the large brick mansion to the front door. He pulled a visiting card out of his case and rang the bell. Without an invitation, he'd have to wait until the hostess received his card and sent a servant back with an answer. The few minutes ticked by slow as the sun rose this late in the year. If Miss Blythe felt indisposed towards their last conversation, she might not wish to entertain him. He hadn't meant to offend her. What could be so personal it'd embarrass her so? Should he ask after the lost item or pretend he didn't remember? Albert decided to keep it to returning the hat and let her choose what else she shared.

"Miss Blythe will see you now." The young maid ushered Albert into the foyer. She collected his hat, gloves, and long coat, but he kept hold of Calista's hat. No doubt his would be brushed and hung near a warm stove ready for departure back into the blustery afternoon.

Calista stood near the settee. "Please do come in and sit down, Mr. Shanahan."

"Thank you for seeing me, Miss Blythe." Her green gown accented lightly with white puffed sleeves accented cascades of curled hair barretted with pearls to frame her ivory face. Albert swallowed hard. He'd get a chance to know her better.

Calista gave him a grand grin. "My hat."

Albert offered it to her. "I thought you might be missing this pretty thing." He couldn't help himself. "I hope to see you wear it again. You looked beautiful in it."

She blushed. "Thank you." Then Calista peeked through her lashes. "I'll be sure to find a reason." She cleared her throat. "Hot cider? We pressed our apples just last week." The blush dissipated as she turned her attention to normal hostessing duties.

He nodded, still standing. "I — uh, I wondered would you speak with me about business for a few moments?" Business? What woman wanted to talk business? How did he not know how to converse with this one lovely lady when he could twist a tornado with anyone else?

She pinked across the bridge of her nose and tipped a nod to the nearby chair. "If you'd be so kind to have a seat, I'll be happy to discuss almost anything with you, sir." Calista laid the hat on a side table.

How many times had she offered him a chair? The other day seeing her in the Gulch didn't seem as awkward as this. But somehow the smaller parlor had an intimate feel to it. The graceful way she moved conjured up imaginings of Miss Calista Blythe entertaining guests in his parlor at his side.

"Ahem," a cleared throat cut in. "Mr. Shanahan, it's a pleasure to see you again."

Albert swiveled. "Please forgive me, Mrs. Blythe. I didn't realize you'd entered."

"Entered? My boy, I've been right here." The elegant lady held out a hand for a welcome. Her eyes twinkled as she glanced between her daughter and Albert. "I believe your attention may have been caught by a brighter flame."

"I can only apologize. I'm carrying a bit on my mind these days. So good to see you again, ma'am."

She smiled and waved away the faux pas. "What is pressing you so strongly, Mr. Shanahan. Is there anything we can do?"

"Actually, ma'am, I believe there is something your daughter might be able to do to help." He sat as the ladies balanced on the edges of their seats, ankles laced neatly to the side.

"What could I possibly do? I mean, of course, within my power I shall do what I can."

"I'm delighted to hear you say so, Miss Blythe."

"Please call me Calista." She leaned forward and touched his arm. "We've been acquainted long enough, don't you think? And should I be granting you a favor, it's quite odd to be so formal."

Her eyes twinkled with good humor much like her mother's. This family passed sweetness down through the generations. Something Albert would very much like for the future generations in his family.

Mrs. Blythe's approving nod relaxed Albert enough to accept the kindness. "Thank you, I'd be delighted. And please, ladies, call me Albert."

"Albert," Calista said, "What would you like to ask me?"

"I hope you'll find it possible to assist me, Calista." The sound of her name rolling off his tongue tasted delightful. "And that you'll approve, Mrs. Blythe, but I've been having a bit of difficulty inviting and finding enough contestants for the Miss Snowflake Pageant."

"How would I be able to help? I don't know anything about

pageants." Calista accepted the tray of hot ciders from the maid. She looked into Albert's face expectantly.

He nodded and took a fine bone china teacup and saucer. She handed a cup setting to her mother as well.

"Miss — Calista," Albert studied her pretty face. The heady aroma of apples and cinnamon stoked his courage. "I seem to need a bit of feminine influence. Many towns started because of gold strikes like our beloved Helena. But eventually the gold runs out like Diamond City." He sipped the steaming sweet liquid letting it warm his belly. "There's nothing left there. It's been less than twenty years since that booming city ruled the territory. I don't want to see that happen to Helena when Last Chance Gulch is abandoned."

"Albert, that wouldn't happen. Not here." Calista's brows drew together as she lightly blew across the surface of her cup. "Surely not here."

"But it could if we're not diligent in building up the city properly."

Mrs. Blythe nodded to Albert. "I've watched it happen time and again. The papers report a strike, and a short time later it's an abandoned town." She sighed. "Yes, it's possible. But what do you think you can do about it, young man?"

"Ladies, in order for a town to grow and prosper, it has to rely on true commerce, industry, and tourism. We need to move away from dependence on gold mining to survive. Our economy must be built on an interconnected society with the rest of the nation — and the world." Albert scooted to the edge of his seat. "We must draw tourism to Helena year round or become yet another town lost to time."

Calista blinked several times as if she digested his announcement. "I see."

"Helena has an amazing abundance of year round opportunity here. Trains come multiple times a day now with reliable service. Since the Hotel Broadwater and natatorium opened the hot springs, it rivals European offerings. But the hot springs mean year round comfort. And our winter sports from skating to sledding delight the hardest of hearts. With a resort like that, and the recognition our society is genteel, cultured, and safe, people will come from around the world to vacation in the Queen of the Rockies. All our businesses will benefit. We have the beginnings of a tourism draw."

"The pageant has to do with all that?" Calista asked, "How?"

"If the young ladies of Helena will help us promote our beautiful city, then we can show the world our society is no longer the Wild West but successfully established. Our ladies feel secure in the streets of Helena, and they will too. Miss Snowflake will help the rest of the world see Montana in a new light. She'll be our ambassador to the world by promoting tourism in our great new state."

"That's rather brilliant, young man." Mrs. Blythe said. "I read about a pageant in Delaware a few years ago. It was quite the hit."

Albert grinned. "Exactly. That's where the idea came from. The people in Rehoboth Beach, Delaware needed year round business. So they created a pageant to draw tourists after the last summer weekend. And they saved quite a few businesses by proving their area had entertainment past summer holidays."

"I understand they've turned that Delaware pageant into a successful annual event." Mrs. Blythe's positive personality added warmth and friendliness to the conversation.

"And you want to do that here?" Calista smiled. "I do love your ingenuity. Isn't he brilliant, Mama?"

He beamed under her compliment. Calista's opinion, above all others, stoked the embers in his heart. "That's what brings me here today." Albert took a deep breath. She'd say yes after all that, wouldn't she? "Calista, would you kindly enter the pageant? I believe if you enter, most of the young ladies in Helena would follow your example. They'd see the event as acceptable." *And I could keep you near while we get acquainted.*

✳

CALISTA SHOOK HER HEAD. She couldn't get distracted from finding Lea a home. "No. I've already told you no."

He looked crestfallen. Calista might have crushed his dream, but she had to save a little girl's future. "I'm sorry. I do believe it will be a successful venture, Albert." She tried to give him an encouraging smile, but she could see the hurt on his face. "I'll be happy to encourage all the young ladies I see."

"I'd hoped your willingness to compete might encourage the other debutantes to join and your family's support would be important to the pageant's legitimacy." He glanced over to her mother and back. "Would you at least consider it?"

She couldn't tell this handsome man she felt called to care for an orphan she'd only met a few days before. To do so would mean outing Lea in front of her mother — and giving her back to a cruel master. Calista wove her fingers together in her lap. "I'm sorry. I don't think I'm the right person to help you with that project."

"Calista," her mother tapped her fingertips on the settee arm. "This might be the perfect way to promote the needs of the orphans you hold dear. Or you could help us promote the vote for women. Either way we can help the orphans."

"Mama, no, I don't think I'm being called to be Miss Snowflake and save our city. There are many more delightful debutantes that deserve the honor more than I."

Albert hung his head. "I understand. But please let me know if you change your mind. Your mother is right. Each young lady will have many opportunities to speak in public about the charity she holds dear. If it's children that touch your heart," and that touched his, "I'm sure you'll be able to reach others for your cause."

Calista caught her bottom lip to keep from blurting out her secret. "If only it were so easy, Albert. Thank you, though, I'm truly honored you think so highly of me. But I think the poor ones on the street need my attention more than my distraction."

Charles stood at the archway. "Miss Calista? That kitten you took a shining to yesterday has disappeared."

"A kitten?" Both her mother and Albert chorused.

Calista jumped in, "It seems the mother abandoned it." True, she hadn't seen the mother cat at all since Lea ruled the carriage house. "I've been terribly worried about its survival." She set her cup down on the side table. "Please forgive me, but I don't want the poor little thing to freeze to death. I'd like to help Charles look for the little critter."

"Calista," her mother frowned. "You dote over much on animals of late." She raised her eyebrows and tipped her head ever so slightly toward Albert.

"May I assist you?" Albert asked.

"It may be the only way to finish your conversation, young man." She shook her head with a disapproving grimace. "Really, Calista, we do have company."

Calista glanced at Charles. His minuscule headshake told her everything. "How thoughtful, but I do believe Charles and I will find it." She smiled and stood. "Thank you for coming, Albert."

He stood and took her outstretched hand. "It's been my pleasure, ladies."

Her mother drew her eyebrows together in a stern, silent glance at Calista. Then she dropped a smile in place for their guest. "Yes, please do come again. You're quite welcome here."

With Albert out the door headed to his rig, Calista whisked up to her room for proper covering. She peeked into each room on the way.

But her mother followed. "One moment, young lady. What in the world has gotten into you today? A lost barn kitten? I do believe that young man has potential. And he seems to place quite high esteem on you."

"Mama, he was quite a little thing." She picked a day coat out of the wardrobe. "I'm sure Mr. Shanahan has a full schedule to keep filling his pageant." She buttoned the long coat. "In fact, I'd be surprised if he wasn't off to the next debutante as we speak."

"Daughter, I think you're missing the point. Albert asked you first. Could it be he has an interest in you other than for his grand idea?"

Calista warmed on the inside. Could it be? Her heart rate beat the question over and over. But all that would have to wait. First, she had a little girl to find. A home to secure for her charge, preferably one that might need a child and a furry black kitten with a sacrilegious name.

CHARLES STOOD in the center of the barn, hands on hips, and a puzzled expression on his face. "We've searched every splinter of the carriage house, Miss Calista. She must have done what she did the other day. Both the heavy rug and the little black kitten are gone."

She'd been using the lap rug as a cape since Calista pinned a brooch or two down the front this morning. At least she had a warm covering. "How quickly can we catch up to Mr. Shanahan?" Calista clasped her hands. "I have no idea how to explain a stowaway in his luggage boot, if that's what she did, but anything could happen if Lea is discovered there before we find her."

"What if I were to ride over to the Tomah Inn and poke about the place?"

"And have you arrested? You'd appear to be criminal." Calista tapped her foot. "I don't know him well enough. He might return Lea to her master, as my parents would do. Then what kind of a beating will she take after days away?" Tears welled up in Calista's eyes. "I don't have enough money to buy her contract unless …" Could she keep a little girl and a kitten hidden for two months? Impossible. But she could have a backup plan — if she couldn't find a home for Lea.

"Should I hitch up the mare?"

"Let's pay Mr. Shanahan a visit at the Tomah Inn. I'll ask him if there's a need for extra hands for the upcoming events while you check the barn area and grounds. That'll give us a good reason to visit." And put my plan into action.

"What if she's not there?"

"Then we can only hope the good Lord has angels watching over her because I can't imagine one more place she could hide. What spooked her this time?"

Charles shook his head. "I think the kitty ran out and she chased after him. I've let her stretch about the place when I'm sure no one is around. I'm terribly sorry, Miss Calista. My heart is sore over the little tyke."

"It's not your fault, Charles. We've undertaken a most unpredictable dilemma. We simply must do the best we can and hope what we're doing is the right thing."

"Sometimes the right thing isn't so easy to decipher." Charles patted Calista's shoulder. "We'll be on our way in a flick of a lamb's tail."

Calista nodded. "Let's find our little lost lamb."

CHAPTER 7

*A*lbert cocked an ear toward the carriage. There seemed to be a squeak as he descended from the step. Better make sure that's oiled up in this weather. He'd brushed down the horse, but hadn't walked far from the carriage house when he spotted the Blythe's man driving up the long lane to the Tomah Inn. He checked for his gloves, hat, and scarf. All there. What besides a forgotten item would bring Charles so quickly 'round?

The carriage pulled to a halt in the common red-bricked yard. A cobblestone here and there looked cracked and a bit worn. "Whoa there, girl." Charles hopped down, still spry for an older man. "Afternoon, Mr. Shanahan." He opened the door for, of all people, Calista.

The kitten! They must think the kitten crawled into his rig. That would explain the soft sound he'd heard. "Calista, what a surprise!"

"Oh do forgive my rush and lack of manners, please, Albert. I wondered if I might speak with you for a moment on behalf of a — friend."

"A friend? I thought you might still be searching for the barn beast. You must have found him?"

"Not quite, but I believe we're close." She smiled and waved Charles away. "May we talk?"

Albert offered his arm. "Please do come in. It's my honor to return your lovely hospitality." He waited as Calista gathered her skirts to walk up the long brick entry with its four risers to the veranda. Then once inside, Albert led her into a comfortable living room. "Tell me, what brings you so quickly?"

"To be honest, I felt uncomfortable asking this of you when I turned down your request. But then I thought it might be doing you a disservice to keep quiet knowing of a possible aid during your busy times."

"What would that be?"

"I know of a young girl who could be very helpful around the house. At this moment, she's indentured. But it's not a pleasant situation."

"I'm sorry to hear that. Please go on."

"Would it be possible that you might need a young girl to clean fireplaces, sweep, help with dishes and changing bedding during the upcoming events?" Calista glanced around the massive meeting room devoid of servants. "I'm not sure how many rooms you have or how many hands you employ, but I thought it might be helpful to share what I knew. I can't imagine the business acumen and organizational skills it takes to run an establishment of this size."

Albert sat taller at the subtle compliment. She admired his abilities and thought enough of him that she wanted to help him succeed. That had to bode well for his desire to know her better. Did this mean she also wished to know him?

"I keep my staff slim, but hire on for special events." No need to share his concerns of future financial failure. He couldn't consider courting until that element resolved anyway. "May I show you around, Calista?" Would seeing the sheer size of the inn scare her off? He'd be wiser to learn that now rather than later, should she accept a request to court him when the time came to ask her father. "We can visit about your friend."

"That'd be a lovely idea. You can tell me about your business." She dimpled up at him.

"Well, we have rooms to host up to twenty in the big house and another four in the guest housing above the carriage house. Although we don't often fill those rooms yet…"

CALISTA WOULD HAVE ENJOYED the tour of the four-story manse except for the missing child. Each flight of stairs led to another incredible discovery of salons, conservatively appointed guest rooms, and the final floor held a massive ballroom the entire length and width of the building with an intricately designed inlaid wooden floor. Windows, arched in graceful sweeping rows, opened onto small balconies overlooking the estate. Diaphanous panels looped over brass rods and tied back to reveal landscaped views below. She could imagine an orchestra playing on the dais while the breeze danced with the lace. Mesmerizing.

Calista peeked out the nearly door-sized window nearest them as Albert turned to explain the difficulty arranging for the grand piano in the ballroom. There she is! Charles chased across the sodden leaf-covered lawn to catch Lea. Calista walked to the piano bench, keeping Albert's attention away from the runaway child below.

"We needed the piano to be disassembled and then reassembled in order to have the instrument brought up all the stairs. But when they sent the workmen, there were only two. Off came the legs. They carted those up easily. But the body of the piano, I was sure it'd end up back down at the bottom, completely destroyed."

Calista laughed. "Ah but it's here, and all in one piece." She touched an ivory key and the high C note echoed through the room. "Wonderful acoustics, Albert."

"Only by the grace of God," Albert chuckled. "As I was

enlisted into helping that day, too. I don't think I've lifted anything quite so heavy in my life. But up three flights —"

She noticed the way his bicep pushed against the woolen weave. Strong arms that could balance a piano would be a safe place for any woman. "I think you are too humble." Calista cleared her throat and walked to the window. She didn't want to see any other woman in Albert's arms. "I believe I should be on my way."

"Of course. I've kept you from your friend."

Calista jumped at the nearness of his voice. She looked up into blue eyes as the flutters returned, tickling her ribs even though her chest couldn't expand. Wasn't she supposed to breathe?

Albert's face softened above hers. "But I'm so glad you stopped by."

"I — I am, too." For a girl schooled in the art of conversation and diplomacy, the lack of intelligence hung on her in Albert Shanahan's presence like a sack of potatoes. She recaptured her thoughts as they descended the grand staircase. "Have you a spot for a house girl?"

Albert's lips angled downward. "I'm sorry, I'm not quite ready to hire anyone else." He glanced at the floor. "I'd like to, but if I may be honest." He lifted his gaze directly into Calista's eyes. "The pageant and tourism are as much for the success of the Tomah Inn as our great state. I don't have room for another employee quite yet. But I hope to one day soon."

Calista knew the idea was a wild hair, but her heart plummeted nevertheless. This would have been a lovely answer for Lea. Obviously not what God had in mind. "Thank you, Albert. I fully understand."

She reached out a gloved hand to wish him goodbye as Lea streaked out from behind a gardening shed. Calista forced herself to remain calm and hide her surprise. Albert would see her and he'd figure out soon why she'd really come! Without a home, Lea needed safety above all things. But she couldn't have that owing an indenture. What if the prize money could free Lea? Calista's mind knit together a plan.

"Albert, does it really mean so much to you to have my participation in the pageant?"

His stunned look riveted on Calista. "Why, yes! You are considered a leading debutante in Helena. Your name is regularly in the society page. Are you —"

Lea plucked up the black kitty and raced toward the shadows of the shed behind this tall, sincere fellow's back.

Keep his attention. Keep his attention. "Yes, um, yes I think I can help you."

"You will?" Albert scooped Calista into a hug and spun her in a circle as Lea disappeared behind the corner.

Calista squealed as she lifted off the ground. She wasn't sure whether the relief of Lea's narrow getaway or the heady feel of Albert's arms around her caused her eyes to close and a small sigh to escape. But when he set her down, her legs trembled.

"I'm so sorry, Calista. I shouldn't have taken that liberty." He flushed as he steadied Calista with hands splayed about her waist. The warmth and strength of his hands soaked through her green silk and velvet suit.

Eyes wide at his spontaneity, and Charles poking his head around the side of the gardening shed to signal he'd captured the quarry, she said, "Perhaps I should fill out your form?" Calista lifted her palms off Albert's strong shoulders and flicked her fingers at Charles to shoo him away.

Confused, Charles scrunched his brows before ducking back.

What must he think? Oh my goodness, what must Albert think of her? Calista wasn't in the habit of being so fresh with any man. But she hadn't asked to be embraced and spun in the air in public — no matter how much she'd enjoyed it.

She wrestled embarrassment as she rustled in her reticule for the ten dollars shopping allowance and the entry card. *Lord, I have no idea how this will turn out. Would you consider this as a tithe and bless it to multiply for Lea's freedom?*

He smiled and offered a pencil and his back for a writing surface. "Thank you."

What had she done?

Albert took the card and money and tucked it into his coat pocket. He walked Calista to her carriage and handed her up into the seat. "I know we're headed toward success now. Be well, and I'll see you soon with an instruction packet."

Where was Lea? What in the world had just happened? The carriage pulled away from the Tomah Inn with Albert standing in the drive. They couldn't stop with him waving them off.

CHARLES PULLED the carriage alongside the road and hopped off the box with agility belying his years. "I'll be with you in a moment, Miss Calista," he called as he walked to the back and then opened the boot. "Out you come, missy."

Calista's words gushed out as Charles plopped the child on the seat beside her. "Oh Charles, I was beside myself worrying about this little scamp. Thank you! However did you manage it?" She brushed back the hair from Lea's face and cupped her chin. "Please don't do that again. Don't run away. I'm trying to help you."

"I didna run away, Miss Calista."

"Then what possessed you to climb into Mr. Shanahan's boot?"

"We was just playin' with the other kitties and somebody came. I did what you said and got meself out of sight. I didna know the coach was gonna go nowhere. Then Jesus kitty got out and I had to ketch him." Her lips trembled. "I won't do it again." She cringed into the corner hugging the well-loved kitty to her chest.

Did she think another switching would come her way? Calista pulled the little girl into a hug. "Oh honey, I'm not mad. I was only worried." She looked over the top of Lea's head.

"Charles, let's get on home and figure out what comes next. She can't keep out of sight forever. We're going to get found out."

His lips drew into a tight line. "I know, Miss Calista. We're going to have to keep puttin' this in the hands of the Lord."

"I believe He has us all in His hands." Calista took a deep breath. "But I also believe God wants us to care for orphans and be obedient. I don't know what to do when those two collide. I'm open to suggestions."

"Sometimes, we just have to take the next step when we don't get to see the whole path. That's trust, Miss Calista, trust. Do you think you can trust God to show you the next step?"

CHAPTER 8

*W*ell if you've given your word, then that's the end of it." Calista's father said.

"I did, Papa. I've given this some thought. Perhaps you were right and if I continue in the pageant, I'll mingle with business owners in the area. Working together, we can find a way to help the children."

Her father rubbed his chin. "If only the poorer children could have the same opportunity to get a good education as the privileged children. We'd clean up the streets and instead of hooligans, we'd have some order."

Calista grinned. Her father loved nothing more than order and law. This tactic led him to the right conclusion. She'd learned her skills of persuasion at his knee. Why, then, did she always feel so inadequate and gauche around certain other women? Catching a glimpse of blond ringlets could still back her into the closest shop to avoid another confrontation. Calista tugged at her inner lower lip with her teeth.

"What else should I be prepared for with this unusual event?"

"Al — I mean, Mr. Shanahan dropped off the information this morning." *He might have dallied a little over tea, Papa, while I noticed the way his laugh sounded.* Calista blinked away the distraction of the handsome Mr. Shanahan's sturdy shoulders shaking at the story she'd told of pumpkin sliding on a frozen lake while at school.

She lifted the packet off her lap. "His plans are for each contestant to perform ..." her voice faltered, "... in public with a Christmas carol." She cleared her throat and continued reading the notes in her hand. "Create a festive store window display to attract shoppers for a local business, and decorate a Christmas tree."

"All are well within your abilities. They should be after all your lessons at Saint Benedict's."

"They are, Papa. That's not the issue. I've learned interior decorating and can use that for the store window treatment, and for the Christmas tree contest—but to perform in public? I don't think that's a good idea. You remember Dora and her trio, don't you?"

"Your mother and I enjoy your performances as do others. You did well at school in elocution and music. I fail to see the dilemma, Calista. Will you really allow an insecure, jealous girl to dictate your future?"

Calista toyed with the fringe on the lamp. "What if she continues to make me look badly? I don't think she's going to stop her gossip."

"Daughter, there'll always be unkind people out to trip you and laugh as you fall. Get back up and hold yourself with dignity. This has gone on far too long. Don't you think others can see through that atrocious behavior? You've given your word. Too late now regardless of any regretful jitters."

"But I'm the one who sang off key." While Dora led the entire recital audience in uproarious laughter — at me.

"If I let other people's behavior stop me because I made a mistake, I'd never follow the path God Almighty set before me. I didn't pass every exam at Yale. One professor threw me out of his class."

"You? But you're a brilliant lawyer!"

"I had a tough time learning all the elements. That professor believed I didn't have what it took. But I didn't quit. Persever-ance led me to be part of history as Montana blossoms into a state." He threaded his fingers together and leaned forward on his elbows. "That professor could have defined my future, if I'd let him. I knew something he didn't. I'd been called to practice law. It was up to me to realize other people do not determine my choices. I chose to discover my strengths and use them."

Calista stared at her successful father. He'd failed? At anything?

"What you choose to do now determines your integrity and your path, not hers. Miss Dora Burdeen must choose for herself as well. I hope she won't decide to base her life around belittling others. How empty and wasted that route would be. Will yours be a path someone else has designed — or the one God has? It's your choice."

"Yes, sir. I know." Calista kissed her father's cheek and left his study.

Calista stared at the floor as she walked to her room. "But I'm still terrified of performing in public, Lord." Calista chastised herself for letting a memory from three years before color her passion to win the funds for Lea's safety. But how would she overcome her fear of embarrassment? Dora also signed up for the pageant, according to Albert, as soon as she heard Calista's name. And she'd coerced the three other young ladies to join her. "Oh, please help me face my fears."

Calista couldn't let go of the memory. Would this be another disaster led by her rival? Whose path would she walk?

THAT NIGHT, once again, Calista snuck out to the small back room in the barn with arms full of clothing. As she turned the lantern up, happy brown eyes sparkled in the glow. Calista's heart warmed at the tiny face grinning up at her. What would it be like to be Lea's mother?

"Miss Calista, Jesus likes me."

"Yes, he does." She grinned back hanging her coat on the back of the door. "Jesus loves all His children."

"No, I mean my Jesus Kitty. He doesn't run off no more." She pointed at the foot of her cot. "See?"

"Oh," Calista laughed. The little girl worked to tame and train the critter all day long since she'd been hiding in the carriage house. "Yes, I do." She reached over to stroke his back. "I imagine all the tidbits he's getting will keep him close."

"But he's real nice now. He follows me everywhere I go. And comes when I call him too! Do you think when you find me a home that I can keep Jesus Kitty?"

How could she guarantee anyone would want to take a child and a barn cat? But the risk of Lea running off would be too great. "I'll tell you what — tomorrow as I'm talking with people in town, I'll keep my ears tuned for someone who needs both a helper and a mouser."

Lea thought deeply before responding. Her head dipped and then she nodded. "Then tomorrows me and Jesus Kitty will work hard on catching mouses. He'll be the bestest mouser you ever sawed."

"I bet he will. Shall we wash you up and feed you some supper?" Calista pulled the warmed bucket of water up onto the corner bench and dropped a cake of soap beside it. "Mr. Charles heated this up so you wouldn't be too cold."

Lea gave the bucket a suspicious glance. "I thought baths were only for Saturdays."

"And for little girls who get new night clothes."

Two brown eyes popped wide. "New?"

"Well, sort of new. I stayed up the last few nights sewing. I hope you won't mind, but I'd outgrown several of my things. I cut down a nightdress and I've been able to almost finish a jumper and blouse." Calista held up the pretty, long-sleeved flannel gown.

"It's so soft." Lea rubbed the pink material and compared it to her rough spun work dress. "It won't be itchy, will it?" Awe tinged her voice.

Calista hadn't thought about how rough and itchy the wool dress Lea wore might feel. Just that she'd been working to come up with presentable clothing should a family want to meet Lea. Clean and well dressed, her chances of an acceptable home would go up.

"After you're all squeaky clean, I need to check the jumper and blouse sizing so I can finish those for you. Then you'll have a new outfit in the morning too."

"I ain't never had a fancy dress like that afore."

"Well, I hope to make a few more for you."

"Miss Calista, who was that man you hugged? Is he a special fella?"

Calista drew in a breath. "You saw that?"

"I wanna fly 'round like that. Would he spin me?"

How did she explain? "Um, that was Mr. Shanahan. Well, you see…" She cleared her throat. "Mr. Shanahan wanted me to join him in an event. He was rather, sort of, happy when I said yes."

"O-o-h." Lea's eyes sparkled. "Did he ask you to get hitched up? My mama said that's a real happy event. My mama said gettin' hitched up was better than gussied up."

Gussied up. That's how Lea's mother explained what she did for a living? "Well, no. He asked me to be in the Miss Snowflake Pageant." *Don't promise what you might not be able to deliver.* Calista measured her words. "I had a hard time making up my mind and finally said yes."

"What cha' 'sposed to do?"

"I decided this afternoon to bake cookies for it. And that's where you come in, little missy. If you're very good, I'm going to need some help. "How would you like to bake gingerbread houses and gingerbread men with me?"

"Cookies!" The words burst from the wriggling little body. "I'll be so, so, so good. You'll see, Miss Calista!"

Lea's short mop of dishwater blond hair washed up easily. Clean, there was a shiny light strawberry glimmer to it. It'd be beautiful grown out without the shaggy choppiness. Her feet were another story. Dirt ground into them without shoes for days left them colorfully embedded with grime. Stockings and shoes had to be next on the emergency list along with a warm coat, bonnet, and gloves. But how to manage all that without being discovered would be another feat of incomparable prowess.

"Miss Calista?"

"Hmm?"

"What ever happened to the Mary lady and the baby Jesus?"

"Where'd we leave off?" She patted small feet dry with a rag. Why not check the attic in the morning for some proper boots? They might be out of style, but didn't Mama keep everything her only child had ever worn for a grandchild one day? She'd have to wait until Mama left for her suffragettes meeting and the maid would go with her for errands.

"Them shepherds visited the manger 'cause the angels told 'em 'bout a baby king."

"Ah, yes." She popped the pink flannel nightgown over Lea's head and helped her clamber into clean drawers fashioned from a left over cotton swatch. Maybe a trunk of old clothing might be stored there too. Handkerchiefs worked well for a nightcap. But unless she found child-sized stockings, a visit to the fabric shop might be the best option.

"Does angels sing for every baby?"

"Uh… " The question hung in the air. Did they? "I don't know."

"I bet my mommy knows. I bet she sings for babies." Lea quieted to a whisper. "Her baby didn't get to breathe so I sang to him when Mama was coughing."

Stinging prickled Calista's eyes and her stomach twisted.

"When your mommy —" She blew out the air she held to release
the building burn in her throat. It took another moment to
swallow the lump before she could finish her question. "When
she passed on, she was having a baby?"

Lea's sad eyes blinked back tears and then she nodded.
"Mama couldn't stop coughing so much so he was borned too
soon. I think he'da been a funner boy. I want a funner playmate."
Silent rivulets ran down her cheeks and down her neck.

Calista wrapped her arms around Lea and held her close. She
began their familiar lullaby to ease the child's suffering. "Away
in a manger, no crib for his bed. The little Lord Jesus lay down
his sweet head…" Bittersweet irony stabbed Calista's heart as she
sang Lea to sleep. So far no one had room for one small child
who'd lost so much.

*Lord, what can I do? Please help me care for this one. This one. But
how can I also care for the many children still without homes? Children
who watch their mommies and brothers die for lack of medicine or food
or care.*

CHAPTER 9

Calista opened the door to the millinery and notions shop, glad to escape the frigid breeze.

Albert shook hands with the merchant who, by the looks of it, agreed to participate in the window decorating competition. "Thank you. With our thirty contestants I'm sure the window displays are going to be a draw for your Christmas shoppers. Here's one of our lovely debutantes now."

The bell over the door tinkled and bumped against the glass as Calista closed it against the wind. She halted as if a driver had pulled hard on her reins. "Mr. Shanahan, I didn't expect to find you here. Hello, Mr. Cooke. Mrs. Cooke." She smiled at all of them.

"How timely. We're —"

The bell jangled again and another young woman entered. Her rust brocade and velvet walking suit complimented light features and upswept hair dangling exquisite ringlets. "Why, Mr. Shanahan, and if it isn't our dear Calista." She bussed a kiss against Calista's cheek. "Hello, Mr. and Mrs. Cooke."

Calista's lips tipped into a wary welcome. "How nice to cross paths, Dora."

"Yes. I've been meaning to visit since you've returned from that…" She paused. "Convent in Minneapolis, was it?"

"While the teachers were nuns, Saint Benedict's is merely a finishing school. I'm sure it's an easy misunderstanding."

"Of course." Dora's eyes glassed over as if she didn't really care to be correct — or corrected. "I'm sure you learned so much more there than you ever could here. At least that's what one could assume since your parents felt the need to send you away. Mine, on the other hand, felt a tutor would best suit while keeping me close and loved."

Calista braved a smile. "I'm sure you also enjoyed a splendid education." Was that an intentional remark meant to make her feel unloved?

"We shall see exactly whose education best prepared her soon, now, won't we?" Dora angled a glance at Calista sideways. Then she bestowed a brilliant smile on Mr. and Mrs. Cooke. "We're proud of our accomplishments here in Helena, are we not?"

The couple gushed to please her. Mr. Cooke offered an elbow. "Would you care to see the new embroidery skeins we have in, Miss Burdeen?" They walked to the next row and chatted over every color in the rack.

Mrs. Cooke, left to tend Calista and Albert, sighed. "Isn't she delightful? We're lucky she chose to join the pageant too, all thanks to you I hear, Miss Blythe. Did you know her embroidery on display in the county courthouse uses our threads?"

Albert nodded. "It's quite a beautiful piece." He turned to Calista. "You should see it. Miss Burdeen created an artistic celebration of Montana's history in a wall hanging."

"I'm sure it's stunning." Calista glanced back toward Dora and caught her watching. Calista chose her words with caution. "I'll have to make a point to view it. Thank you for telling me."

"My pleasure. I think you'll enjoy the artistry." He paused. "Do you enjoy art, Miss Calista?"

Surprised at his question, she stammered, "Why yes. Though

I'm not as capable in embroidery to call it art. I prefer musical instruments." Now why had she brought up music? If Dora heard —

"I do remember your penchant for singing. So quaint, really." Dora sashayed up the aisle with a basket of colorful skeins in hues of greens and reds. "With your love of music, I'm sure you had opportunity to pursue it since you last performed. Did your esteemed school help you improve?"

Calista's face heated. She repeated her father's words in her head. *Hold yourself with dignity and follow your own path.* Calista took a breath. "If I didn't, at least I can enjoy myself." *Change the subject, Calista. Don't let her get your goat.* "I hear you're quite the artisan with embroidery."

"Yes, thank you. I enjoy designing beautiful things." She lowered her lashes. "I'd be happy to teach you."

"Thank you, no, I believe I'll leave it to you artists." Calista smiled. Did the smile reach her eyes? "My talents are elsewhere. I have a little knitting to do, though, for a few gifts."

"Ladies, this store will be participating in the window dressing for the Miss Snowflake Pageant. Since you're both patrons, would one of you like the honor?"

Mrs. Cooke watched the two ladies with deep interest. She'd be sure to have enough fodder for her friends after this afternoon if they added sparring over the notion shop windows.

"I think —" Calista started to offer Dora the honor.

"How utterly perfect for me," Dora laid her fingers on Albert's sleeve.

Calista's throat went dry at the sight of Dora and Albert so close together. What was it about seeing Dora's hand on Albert's arm that bothered her? It was a casual gesture, wasn't it?

"Don't you think so, Mr. and Mrs. Cooke?" Dora swiveled her head to encompass the couple.

Mrs. Cooke nodded while Mr. Cooke grinned beside her. "We do," Mrs. Cooke agreed.

"Wonderful, that's solved." Albert turned to Calista. "I'll be in touch with your assigned shop window soon then." He collected his coat and excused himself. "Miss Dora, Miss Calista."

Was that a hint in his voice for a repeat tea? Calista's heart pitter-pattered. She squeezed her fingers together inside the fur muff. Concentrate. Dora — the last person who should discover Calista's secret.

Mrs. Cooke asked, "Now that's settled, what may I help you with, Miss Blythe?"

No more itchy clothing for Lea. "Soft, heavy yarn for stockings, please." Since Dora didn't seem to be leaving any time soon, Calista would choose her yarns and needles and be on her way. She'd have to guess at the pattern. She couldn't safely purchase one for a child, not with a very nosy Nellie hawking after her through the store.

"I'd like one each of a navy, a white, and a gray for now." Three sets of stockings should suffice for the moment to go with the dresses and coats from the attic. She hoped Lea would have a home long before she'd need more. But little girls still needed Christmas gifts, if the new family didn't mind.

Mrs. Cooke returned with the requested items. "Here we are, Miss Blythe. Will these do?"

Calista fingered the lovely skeins. Soft as Jesus Kitty's fur. A smile twitched at her lips. Now that would set Dora's tongue to tinder. "Quite nicely, yes. Thank you."

"They're very soft. And the needles you chose are fine. Can you knit?" Dora fingered the yarn on the counter. "What are you going to make with them?"

Rather than get into what she could and couldn't do, Calista shrugged and forced herself not to snatch the yarn away. "I thought I'd try my hand at socks." Calista had learned intricate knitting designs in her homemaking classes. She'd be able to turn out a pair of simple long socks for Lea quickly. With private time, possibly by tomorrow. She'd have to add a little thickness in the foot to help the old boots fit better, though.

"Very practical." She nodded, but Dora's tone said she thought socks mundane.

"Yes, sometimes a gift is best when it meets a need."

"Someone you know needs stockings?"

Oh dear, she'd said too much. She needed to divert attention quickly. Calista shrugged again, this time to buy time, as her stomach flipped. "Doesn't everyone? But I'm not going to take a chance that someone will find out my gifts. So you won't mind if I don't tell who I'm making the gifts for, will you?"

Dora's cold smile froze. "Of course, keep your secrets. We wouldn't want to spoil someone's Christmas morning receiving..." She scrunched her nose. "...socks now, would we?" She gave a light giggle as if she'd acquiesced to a private joke.

"Let me wrap those for you," Mr. Cooke interjected. "Did either of you hear about the lost little indentured girl?"

Mrs. Cooke added. "I sure hope she's holed up somewhere safe. Those clouds looked ominous this morning."

Calista edged away from the counter with her purchases.

"That man of Chicago Joe's about given up now it's been two weeks," Mrs. Cooke added. "But I wish they wouldn't stop looking. We've just been so worried."

With as loud and thorough as he'd been, the man made sure everyone in town knew Lea had run away. Now how would Calista find a safe place for her? The moment Lea turned up, she'd be returned to Chicago Joe's establishment. What family would hinder the richest woman in Helena? For that matter, even with what she did for business, Chicago Joe had helped too many or done favors for that many and then some. Now what? How would she look outside of Helena for a loving home?

"I don't wish any ill on the child, but why all the fuss?" Dora asked. "There are street children everywhere. Surely she's being hidden by someone or—"

Calista's sharp intake of breath didn't go unnoticed.

Dora focused on Calista. "Did you hear something about her?"

"Me?" Calista stalled. What could she say?

"That's what I asked."

"Only what you've heard." That was true. This was the first time she'd heard anything more. "I just can't imagine such a small child being so scared she'd run away. It must have been a terrible situation. What can we do for these children?"

"Hmm. I wouldn't know," Dora said. "It's really not our problem."

"Those nuns might have her over at the House of the Good Shepherd. And if they did, she'd be safe enough," Mr. Cooke offered. "I don't think the authorities would challenge the Catholic Church for a runaway indentured servant. Especially one so young, if the reports are correct. Chicago Joe might be convinced to consider the indenture contract as a donation."

Calista hadn't thought of the home for wayward girls. The nuns at Saint Benedict's had been tough disciplinarians, but that helped her learn self-discipline as well as several languages and instruments, the beauty of being a faith-filled woman in God's plan, and management of large properties — not to mention her artistic skills with threads, yarns, and paints. Could that kind of an education be available for Lea? And solve the financial issue?

Her thoughts spun from what would happen to Lea if she were discovered to the possibility of an excellent education with the nuns. Would she be able to take Lea to the House of the Good Shepherd? Would Lea be safe there? Or would the nuns feel required to turn her over? Calista's heart squeezed.

CHAPTER 10

*C*harles handed Calista down from the carriage in front of the convent on Hoback Street. "We'll be waiting around the corner on Ninth. When I see you come back out, I'll pull the old girl forward."

"Thank you, Charles. I'm a bit nervous to leave Lea anywhere in town, but with you I'm certain she'll be fine." Calista ducked her head back in the carriage door.

The little girl wore a gray dress, matching coat, and a shoulder cape trimmed with light blue fur. Her light gray stockings were the first pair Calista finished. The little black boots fit well with the thicker footies knit two layers deep instead of one. "Please stay put, Lea. I'll come back soon."

Bonnet already askew despite the light blue bow tied under her chin, the little girl swung her feet off the edge of the leather bench. "I gots Jesus Kitty to keep me com-pny." The kitten hopped off her lap onto the other seat. Lea scrambled across the bench after him.

Charles snapped the door shut. "I'll keep both little critters safe and contained, Miss Calista."

"Oh I hope the House of the Good Shepherd won't turn away the kitten. She's grown so attached," Calista whispered to

Charles. She sighed. "It doesn't much matter though, does it? We have to do the right thing for her whether they take the kitten or not."

Charles face suddenly looked a bit older as he whispered back, "I'll sure miss her." He patted Calista's shoulder. "But it has to be."

"It has to be." Calista straightened her shoulders and marched herself up the steps. She closed her eyes and knocked.

It wasn't long before a young lady in a school uniform opened the door. "Hello? May I help you?"

"Hello, I have a rather delicate situation. May I speak to the Mother Superior privately, please?"

"Won't you come in?" She held the heavy door back as Calista entered. "I'll ask if she can see you. Please be seated."

A few minutes later the girl brought back the Mother Superior. "I understand you've asked to speak with me?" She dipped her veiled head to the young girl. "Thank you, Veronica, you may return to your afternoon chores."

Veronica curtsied. "Yes, Mother."

Calista curtsied as well before she spoke. "It's rather a difficult errand that brings me. One needing the utmost discretion."

"You may have it. Here at the House of the Good Shepherd our goal is to help young women, not cause them further grief. Are you Catholic, my dear?"

"No, Mother, but the difficulty is not mine. It's a young child I'd like to speak with you about."

"Come to my office, and we'll discuss the dilemma." She led the way to a sparsely appointed room with a desk, two chairs, and a bookcase with school texts and several Bibles. A simple wooden cross hung on the wall behind her desk.

"You may speak freely here, child."

She sat on the edge of the shallow chair to allow her small bustle space. Calista wasn't sure how to start. "I understand you're able to take in girls who are in trouble."

"Yes, we house several young ladies and help them learn a trade so they can survive on their own one day."

A trade! Safety and a way to support herself as Lea grew older. That'd be perfect. She'd never have to go back to work for a house of ill repute. Even one hiding behind the façade of a variety theater like Chicago Joe's. "I've run across a young girl in town who I think needs your help. Unfortunately, she's run from a cruel and unfair indenture."

"How old is she?"

"I believe she's around six."

"While that's a very young age for an indentured servant, she's still too young to be accepted here with us. An orphanage would be better until the child is old enough to attend classes. You see, all our girls must attend school or work and are at least the age of eight and on into adulthood."

"But, I'm afraid something horrible will happen if she is left on the streets. Please, isn't there something you can do?"

"We will pray. But our calling is not to be an orphan home. I understand that is to come still. Our purpose is to educate young ladies to become productive members of society." She folded her hands on the desk. "I'm terribly sorry we can't help you unless you'd like a letter of introduction to a home further east."

"I don't know what to do to help her." Calista's words trembled.

"Perhaps the Lord will show you, if you'll be open to His leading." The nun's lips hinted at a smile. "Perhaps it is she who is to help you."

Help me? What in the world did that mean? But still there would be no home for Lea. Only the very real game of hide and seek that couldn't go on much longer without being uncovered. "Mother, I'd like that reference letter, please."

She inclined her head. "You may return next week." The nun tinkled a small bell on her desk.

Calista opened her mouth to point out time was of the

essence then snapped it shut. With one emergency option open for Lea, alienating the mother superior didn't seem wise.

Veronica reappeared to show Calista the way out of the convent. Such a safe place, so full of peace — and yet no safety here for Lea. Calista's heart churned. At least she hadn't blurted out her name or that she was hiding the child in her carriage house.

LIST COMPLETED and display windows assigned, Albert spent the morning crafting thirty postcards with the simple contest rules and tucked them into a briefcase. The ladies would have two weeks to design and execute Christmas windows for each of the thirty businesses.

Albert turned his horse in at the Child Carriage House while he went about errands downtown. First he employed several newsies hanging out on corners nearly done with their paper duties. A coin or two and the boys went off delivering notes to all the remaining contestants with their assigned businesses for the holiday festivities. Window dressing would not only show off the debutantes decorating skills, but had to cause a stir as a Christmas Village extravaganza appeared in the heart of Helena, Montana. Why hadn't he kept one debutante's card and delivered it to her himself? Albert mentally shook himself. A missed opportunity!

Albert stopped at the Independent to work with the reporter on an article inviting the community to take part in the Christmas Village displays and the events of the Miss Snowflake Pageant.

"This sounds like a society page piece to me." The reporter pulled a pencil from behind his ear. "Tell me the highlights."

Albert thought for a moment. "Our contestants will need votes as they create a Christmas Village in downtown Helena. Residents and visitors will drop a card in the collection boxes, inside the businesses, for their favorite window display. The lady with the most cards will win the first event leading up to our Miss Snowflake Pageant to be held on Christmas Eve at the Broadwater Hotel and Natatorium."

"This sounds like quite an undertaking, Mr. Shanahan. And at the Broadwater, no less! Should be quite a to-do. I heard Mr. Broadwater say he was draining the natatorium."

"Yes, since he promised to lay a dance floor for the Governor's Inaugural Ball, I managed to secure a test of the floor by staging the final events of the pageant there. With the crowds drawn to the pageant, many will rent rooms and take the private baths."

"You're a thinker, Mr. Shanahan, yes sir, quite a thinker! I was at the Governor's swearing in. But Mr. Broadwater hasn't yet announced a date after declaring his plans. I imagine the legislature's dissolving into disagreements last week doesn't help much."

"I read about that." Albert leaned on his elbow, listening to the man's firsthand account.

"Those republicans and democrats can't sit down and talk for beans." He shook his head. "Why no politician has any common sense is beyond me. Blustering and yelling like you've never heard. They can't agree because they can't hear each other talking over the chaos." He slapped a hand on the polished counter. "People on the streets act like that and they'd end up in jail for disorderly conduct. A few of those gents need a night to cool off. There'd be a piece of news! But I just report the news, I don't make it." He shook his head.

Albert laughed. "And they thought the Wild West was all about the Indian Wars and the vigilantes. I'd say it's about our polished politicians nowadays. What say you and I make it about taking a beautiful winter holiday in our lovely state instead? Something to help Montana stand out for the right reasons."

"You say this Miss Snow — what'd ya' call her?"

"Miss Snowflake. Her job is to promote Montana tourism so we have businesses when the gold runs out."

"I think we're already well into a dry up. But I imagine the whole town will turn out to see the Christmas Village." The reporter licked the lead of his pencil, leaving a dark line, and dropped it to his notes. Then he peered up through round spectacles. "When is it, you say?"

Albert pointed at the calendar. "Saturday, December seventh, Christmas village window walking tour. Ribbon cutting to start the festivities at one o'clock sharp."

"Do you have anything else to add?"

"How about all our lovely debutante contestants will be along the walking tour talking about their displays? Votes will remain open for two weeks and gathered for a count. Other contest events will include an ice skate party and music performances." He thought for a moment. "How about we do another article for the gala and crowning?"

The reporter nodded. "Want to mention any participating merchants?"

"That'd be a nice touch, wouldn't it?" Albert pulled out his list. "What do you think of running their names? I have the New York Store, First National Bank, both dry goods stores. With the Clarke, Conrad, and Curtin Store as well as the Helena Furniture Store and, though the Windsor Hotel is a bit further down Main Street, they've asked to be included."

"I'm glad for such a pleasant article after the way those politicians have behaved. That should work into a nice write up, Mr. Shanahan. I'll see what I can do to get these business folks sponsoring a few advertisements for the event. How would that be? Good for you and good for me. Can't beat good business, right?"

"That's a fine idea. Now let's hope those windows really do create a Christmas village wonderland. Somehow we need to bring a lot more cold weather commerce before we all dry up like the mines are starting to do."

CHAPTER 11

*T*he lad grinned through his freckles at the extra penny and the hot biscuit Mrs. Brown pressed into his hands. "There you go, boy. Thank you for your trouble."

Calista watched the kindness unfold on her kitchen stoop.

"Thank you, ma'am." He ate half on the spot in two gulps.

"Go on now, eat the rest." Calista urged. "Mrs. Brown is the best cook in the state." She grinned at the housekeeper.

"No, miss, thank you." The boy shrugged. "My little brother needs somefin', too, t'day."

Mrs. Brown's smile flopped as if she'd flattened a soufflé. Spatula in her hands and picking up the tray, she asked, "Won't you get some dinner at home?"

He clamped his mouth shut and paled as he backed away from the door.

"Wait! Would you like some more biscuits, boy?" Calista called.

The boy stopped and turned. "I could … have another?"

Calista pulled out a sheet of waxed paper and laid it on the table. "How about some for you and some for your brother?" At a nod from Calista, Mrs. Brown slid half a dozen white fluffy buttermilk biscuits onto it. Calista pulled up the corners and formed a packet.

As she handed it to the boy, she said, "Maybe they'll keep your hands warm for a short time." Then she winked at him.

He jumped up and down and set out at a brisk walk to find his little brother.

"Looks like he thinks they're feasting tonight." She sighed. "Another homeless one. I wish there was something I could do. There seems to be even more children in the streets since the trains keep coming."

"You've done what you could." The wise woman consoled Calista. "That's all anyone can do. They'll have a biscuit for Thanksgiving tomorrow, too." Mrs. Brown put an arm around Calista. The women watched the boy whistle until he disappeared down the drive.

"Mrs. Brown, will you have enough to pack a picnic basket for Mama still? That's what I came to tell you. The women suffragettes are going to meet over lunch at the Broadwater Hotel so Mama will be gone this afternoon."

"Oh don't you fuss a bit of it. I have lots of other tidbits made up already." She bustled about the kitchen loading a jar of pickles, slicing homemade bread, and popping in a can of potted meat followed by a ball of cheese rolled in nuts, dried apples, and topped it off with apple turnovers.

"That almost makes me wish I was going." Calista grinned at the older woman then picked up the card the boy had delivered. "I've been assigned the Gold Block building to decorate the windows facing out on Main Street."

"My, oh, my." Mrs. Brown tucked the plaid tablecloth around the foodstuffs, plates, and sundry in the basket. "Sounds like a lot of work."

"But I think that newsie gave me an idea. Maybe there's a way to at least get people thinking about the children."

❄

GINGERBREAD COOKIES COVERED EVERY SURFACE. Calista cut out gingerbread men, horses, and bells and then slid another tray into the oven.

"How did you like your Thanksgiving supper, Lea?" Mrs. Brown asked. "Did Mr. Charles get it to you while it was still warm?"

"Oh ma'am, I ain't never sawed so much food!" Her eyes were big and shining with joy.

"I'm so glad you enjoyed it."

"Mr. Charles, he done brung a plate out and ate it all up with me and Jesus Kitty." Lea gave a giggle. "Jesus Kitty likes meat and spuds and gravy like I do!"

Mrs. Brown sent Calista a look of consternation, "I can't get used to that name for a cat, but I'm sure glad to hear you both enjoyed your feast."

"Can I do the frosting?"

"You stir hard like so." Mrs. Brown handed a bowl of frosting over to Lea. "You try."

Lea's arms, stronger from the weeks of nourishment, still struggled with heavy decorator's icing. She couldn't quite hold the large bowl and move the wooden spoon in circles at the same time. The spoon flipped up leaving a glob smeared on small knuckles.

"Are you going to let it go to waste?" Mrs. Brown feigned a scolding.

Lea caught on, but watched cautiously as she tasted the white wonder. Then a giggle erupted as she licked her frosting covered fingers. "I've never tasted anything so good."

Calista drew her brows together as she glanced over from the marble pastry counter. "You've never had a cookie before?"

"Uh uh." She waggled her head back and forth. "I heard of 'em though."

"We'll save some so you can have another now and then. But let's get these horses frosted first." The little girl had filled out a bit over the last few weeks. Her cheeks looked rosy instead of sunken.

Lea danced her horse-shaped cookie on the sugar pile used to dip the cutters in before pressing the dough. "This here is Sugar Dance. She's a special pony."

Calista handed a frosting spade to Lea. "That's the perfect name for a ginger cookie horse." She picked up another cooled cookie to frost herself.

"What's yers called?"

Calista cocked her head and thought for a moment. "What do you think of Rosebud? Wouldn't she be pretty on a carousel?"

"Oh yes, Miss Calista. Sugar Dance and Rosebud are bestest friends."

The child earned a chuckle from both women.

"How many children do you think never tasted a ginger cookie or have regular meals, Mrs. Brown?"

She clucked her tongue while retying the slipping dishtowel around Lea's waist. "I can't imagine." Her eyes remained on the diminutive confection chef. She crooked her head toward Lea. "But what are you going to do with this sugar princess?" She tickled Lea's ribs, enticing a happy shriek.

Calista met the cook's eyes. "I'm working that out."

"Are you really? Because she needs parents, not a mish-mash of a housekeeper, a driver, and a young lady without a husband." She smoothed down her own apron. "If it weren't for your parents busy with the women's vote and Mr. Charles keeping this little cookie out of the way when they're home …" She lifted her brows.

"I know."

"This can't go on forever. Someone is bound to figure out why there's always a bit extra after every meal."

"I've set my mind to win the contest. I have to. The only way to get her a home is to make sure she's legally free. I'll pay off her indenture and then the letter of recommendation from the nuns will let me take her back East to a reputable orphan home— "

Calista looked at Lea. What would she be like when she grew up? What would happen to her so far away? *Or I could find a husband. What would make a man like Albert, or any man, want a street child?* "Or we start a home right here."

"An orphan home, here? How in the world do you propose to get something like that built?"

"Mrs. Brown," Calista leaned back against the counter. "The only thing I know right now is I'm taking one step at a time." She flicked a hand toward the back door where the newsie scarfed down the biscuit. "But you and I both know the orphan issue around here isn't getting better. With Helena being the last stop for the orphan trains, too many children are not being placed in homes. They just land on our streets. Somebody has to do something or—"

Lea looked between the women. Her lips scrunched up in a red face like she held back a wail. "I don't wanna go."

Calista cupped her sugar-covered cheeks, "You, sweet thing, are very special. We are going to find the perfect home."

"Do I have to go away?" She held a half-eaten gingerbread man with frosting oozing up between her fingers.

"Just to the bath right now. We have a short time before the rest of the household comes back from their appointments." Calista untied the dishcloth and handed it off to Mrs. Brown. "Let's clean you up and back to your play spot. Shall we?"

"I thought baths were only on Saturdays."

"And little girls covered in stickies." Calista giggled as she tapped a fingertip on Lea's frosting-tipped nose. "I'll be back to help in a few minutes, Mrs. Brown."

"I'll finish frosting these gingerbread men. You get on with that so she isn't discovered, and I don't lose my job for my part in this fiasco."

Calista stopped short as she heard Mrs. Brown's words. *Could the choices I'm making cause harm to either Mrs. Brown or Charles?* She turned with wide eyes and stared at the frank woman. "I—"

"Get on with you." Mrs. Brown shooed her up the stairs. "I

chose to be part of this. I know the consequences. Her dinner will be waiting behind the breadbox."

Calista whisked Lea in and out of her first real tub bath in record time. She had to have her safely scrubbed, dressed, and playing in the carriage house before she put the jobs of caring people at risk — people she'd known all her life. People willing to take huge risks for a child they hadn't even known three weeks ago.

Charles had nonchalantly met the carriage further from the stable door. What if her father suddenly decided to inspect the horses and equipment?

What if her mother noticed the clothes missing from the attic trunks? Or the odd pilings of yarns and notions lying about Calista's room? Hadn't she already asked why the lamp stayed on so late? Calista could only claim insomnia a few times before it became suspicious.

CHAPTER 12

*D*ora's window display at the milliner's shop looked ethereal with the mild sunshine lighting outside the shadow of the blue awning. She'd followed the theme of a Christmas village to perfection.

"Lovely, isn't it? To be able to see what the shops offer," Albert asked Calista as he ducked under the awning in front of the brick building. "I do believe the construction of the window villages is as much a draw as the parade down Main Street to see the finished scenes will be."

Calista offered a gloved hand in greeting. "I've been admiring the displays as the girls have been building them. Such beautiful handiwork and interior design ideas." And tough to avoid being seen in her daily adventures. But she'd pretended to watch as scenes in the windows developed to give her a reason to stroll looking for hungry children.

Crinkles lit up Albert's eyes and a dimple deepened each cheek. "Since many of the businesses installed new plate glass windows the last few years, they open up the storefronts. That's what gave me the idea for this part of the competition. Until the trains came, we didn't have such niceties."

"Yes, the trains changed everything." Should she add a toy

train with an adorable gingerbread man conductor? Without them the last six years, life in Montana would most definitely be one of continued deprivation. The trains brought civilization. Calista turned back to the panorama behind glass. "And I do believe Miss Burdeen is going to be the one to beat."

White cotton batting mimicked snow gently rolled in small hills and valleys. Tea cozies embroidered to look like houses stretched over china teapots dotting the simulated snow-covered hills. Thimbles set on small ribbon spools resembled a tiny tea party in the center of the china village. Crocheted snowflakes hung from thread all through the window. But on closer inspection, the snowflakes also had tiny crystal beads that caught the light as they spun in the air.

"She's been adding to her village scene almost every day. It's going to be a draw during the festival judging." He nodded as he said, "Exactly what I hoped for, as are so many of the other window scenes. We'll have Helena and surrounding towns coming just to tour Main Street for our Miss Snowflake Christmas Village parade."

Would hers please Albert as much? It seemed very different than the rest. But then starting over because the display had been devoured wasn't likely a problem for the other contestants.

"How is yours coming along, Miss Calista?" His voice carried a tinge of concern. "I haven't seen it started yet."

Oh once or twice. A grin tickled her cheeks. But Calista bit her tongue before the words popped out. "I'm heading there now to meet Charles. He's unloading the carriage for me." She smiled. "A last errand to run first." Calista patted her large basket. She'd have started two days ago if she hadn't spotted the same newsie, Frankie, and his little brother.

Two hungry boys soon built to more than a dozen trickling by the carriage. Instead of gingerbread men in a miniature rendition of Helena as the gingerbread village, Calista had handed out every crumb as more and more children found out the cookies existed. They poured out of every nook and cranny along Last Chance Gulch.

The real, live hungry tummies overruled the need to decorate a display that represented those real, live children. Mrs. Brown cautioned her. "You have to be sure to get the display built this time if you want to help those rascals long term." Then she promptly set about making the dough for dozens more houses and cookie men.

"I will." Calista donned an apron and went to work alongside the other woman. They rolled, cut, baked, and frosted the village pieces. Lea sneaked in to help again while Mrs. Blythe spent the afternoon on social visits and Mr. Blythe worked at his offices in town.

The next day both women filled every available basket with new creations. Lea played in the loft with her kitten while Charles mended harnesses. He'd keep the two little scamps busy and out of sight.

"I'll put these little buildings in the window for the village." Calista gently placed a large square gingerbread building, glued together with stiff, dried frosting, and iced to look like one of the banks into a box of popcorn. "That should keep it safe for the trip. We can add the gingerbread boys over the next few days."

"There's a bag of bruised apples from the cellar. They won't store well. With all the hubbub, I'm just not going to get to jelly making in time. I've had Charles stow them in the carriage for you. I'm sure they'll be put to good use."

"Mama." Calista kissed her mother's cheek when she entered. "I'm just heading into town to work on my window."

"Didn't you do that the other day?" She perused the remaining cookie art. "My, but these are well done. Such pretty lacy roofs and goodness, I can tell which building is which!"

"It took a lot more time than I'd expected." Calista skirted the original question. "Do you need anything while I'm there?"

"No, dear, I've come for some tea." She turned to Mrs. Brown.

"Did I hear you say we have a bag of spoiling apples? Seems our food stuffs are going a bit quicker than usual this year."

Calista busied herself putting on her coat, buttoning it up, checking her pockets for gloves. Anything to avoid looking at her mother.

"Do you mind sending the apples in for charity, ma'am? I seem to recall that's what you had me do in the past."

Calista held her breath and silently cheered Mrs. Brown's quick thinking. She tied the blue velvet bonnet in place, checking to be sure the hat wouldn't dislodge this time. The wide brim should shield her from sudden gusts. Now why did that incident come to mind?

"No, not at all. It's not a good steward that lets his stores go to waste, now is it?" Mrs. Blythe answered. "Will you have time to do that with your plans, dear? It seems you've been quite busy lately with the snow contest."

"They're calling it a pageant, Mama. We have several areas of competition. This is just the first, creating a Christmas village window scene." Calista smiled conspiratorially at Mrs. Brown. "I'd be happy to help take care of those apples, Mama. Happy to." She kissed her mother's cheek again and winked at Mrs. Brown as she dashed out the door before any further questions could arise.

On the street now with Albert, Calista shifted the weight of the apple basket.

"That seems heavy." He offered a hand. "May I carry it for you?"

How would she hand out the fruit unnoticed with someone in tow? Calista pulled back. "No, but thank you." She smiled to soften the refusal. "I have it."

"She's here!" A lad called down the block and pointed at Calista. "Look, she's by the sewing shop!"

Albert snapped to attention, searching for the shouter. "He's pointing at you." He stepped in front of her and pressed her back toward the doorway of the shop.

There'd be no way to do this secretly any longer. At least nine or ten newsies raced toward them, hats grasped in hands so as not to lose them while socks slid down and knickers slipped up to show knobby knees. She sidestepped around Albert.

"What are you doing?" He held Calista back by dropping an arm in front of her. "Go in the shop. I'll take care of whatever this problem is. I won't have my, er, my pageant contestants accosted in the streets. These youngsters are getting quite bold."

His instinct to protect a lady sent a shiver of admiration through Calista. But there was no need to protect anyone. "No. I know what this is, Albert. They're coming to see me."

The boys, hopping the trolley rails and dodging pedestrians who observed window display creations in progress, nearly landed in a heap at Calista's feet. "Did you bring more cookies, miss?" Freckle-faced Frankie whooshed out for the lot of them.

Albert's hands spread wide encompassing the crowding boys. "What is this?" he boomed.

The boys all shrank backward but glued their eyes on Calista's basket.

Calista watched all their faces fall. She put a hand on Albert's arm. "It's really all right."

"Boys, you can't come rushing at people." Albert crossed his arms. "You're going to cause a panic running around like a gang."

"Sorry, mister. We weren't gonna hurt nobody," Frankie answered. Several others hung their heads and murmured apologies. But none left.

Calista appreciated the firm manner Albert used to get the group under control. It wouldn't do to have them gang up on her in the streets, no matter how innocent. Someone else might take it for an attack or panhandling. These boys needed a man to teach them the things of life and a little discipline. They had so much to learn beyond selling papers on street corners to survive one more day. *Lord, please show me a way to change these lives.*

"No, Frankie, I didn't bring cookies today." A chorus of disappointment followed. Then she swept back the cloth covering her basket. "But I did bring apples. I hope I have enough for all of you."

The boys cheered. "Real apples! Apples, apples, apples!"

She chanced a glance at Albert. His astonished expression made him look like a vaudeville actor from the theatre across the road. What was he thinking?

"You're feeding the newsies?"

"They're hungry. Some of the boys have homes, but this bunch, I don't think so. Frankie," she tossed a smile and an apple in the boy's direction, "told me they try to get one meal a day off their earnings."

Conflicting emotions flickered across Albert's face. His eyes squinted at her as if he couldn't quite peg her.

Calista expected Albert to disapprove. To stop the apple-fest. But rather than shoo the boys away, Albert stuck a hand in and pulled out two apples.

"Here boys, who wants an apple?"

Hands shot up all around them. "Me!"

"Me too, mister!"

As Albert tossed apples to outstretched hands, he asked, "None of you boys have homes?"

Frankie spoke for the group, his voice a tad defensive. "We got homes, mister. They jes ain't in big, fancy houses like you folks got." Rubbing his apple across his belly, he said, "No offense, Miss Calista." He chomped into the apple, bruise and all.

"None taken, Frankie."

Albert cocked his head, "No offense intended on my part either, young man."

Frankie shrugged and mimicked Albert's words. "None taken, sir." Then he straightened his shoulders as if he'd granted a grand pardon.

Calista covered a laugh with a cough behind her hand. She'd be careful not to chip a hole in his pride. For the moment, it seemed all these boys had — that and the pittance earned as newsies passing out the Independent's daily papers.

A few more boys straggled to the back of the bunch. "Did she bring biscuits or cookies this time?" one whispered.

Albert speared Calista with an intense gaze. "How long have you been doing this?"

She swallowed. "Since Frankie and I made friends." She'd been so careful not to be noticed pressing a cookie or bun into a hand as she passed. But until today, she'd wandered the sidewalk and handed out a treat one-by-one. The cookies, and her regular presence, seemed to be something the boys watched for in the afternoons.

"And how did you—" Albert snapped his fingers and pointed at the freckled face of the lanky pack leader. "Frankie, did you deliver a note to Miss Blythe a week or two ago?"

"Yes, sir." Frankie's eyes widened. He looked like wary fox caught by a farmer in the henhouse. "I did jes as you asked. I didn't do nothin' wrong. I didn't ask for a tip, or nothin'."

"I see." Albert nodded and rubbed his chin.

"Then she done let me have some biscuits for me an' my little brother." Frankie thumbed a gesture toward a smaller, less freckled child. "I had enough to share with Tom and Bo."

The entire group of boys looked to range from about six or seven to young teens. Frankie seemed to fit somewhere in the middle. But Frankie had leadership qualities.

"If I'm to understand, all you boys know Miss Blythe? She's fed all of you cookies, biscuits, and, uh, apples a few times?"

Rounds of nods and a "Yes, sir," competed with apple juice dribbling on chins.

Calista flipped the cloth back over the empty basket. "Listen, Albert, if this is a problem for—"

"I'm overwhelmed. I just don't know how you and your parents can keep it up with this many mouths to feed." He took a head count as the newsies jostled each other for a spot in her company. "There's over a dozen here now."

Her parents? Calista's eyes widened. No, no, no. Now what? He was sure to mention the odd street ministry. How could she keep her activities under wraps? But more to the point, how could she keep feeding these children?

She turned to the boys and handed out a few extra apples from her pockets that hadn't fit the basket. "Give these to someone in need. I'll see what I can find for tomorrow. But until then, please be careful." She'd explain and ask for discretion. Surely a gentleman wouldn't discuss an act of charity as gossip. If he did, could she keep the topic to the apples? Her mother all but told her to give them away.

The jovial cluster of orphaned newsboys began to break up with shouts of thanks, promises to come the next day, and elbows playfully jabbing ribs back-and-forth.

"Won't those boys just keep the extras?"

"You'd be surprised at how they look out for one another. Right, Frankie?"

Frankie popped a strong nod, "Yes, ma'am, we do." He threw an arm around his little brother. "Say yer thanks, Joey."

"Thank you, mith." Missing a front tooth, the boy's adorable lisp flipped Calista's heart. He must be around Lea's age. Then he tugged on Frankie's hand. The two scurried off toward the south end of the gulch.

A woman's voice broke into the sound of scuffling feet. "Well now, whatever is happening here?" Dora swished her skirts away from the boys darting past her. She held her gloved hand against her nose as if the boys' stench affronted her sensibilities.

CHAPTER 13

*D*ora wrinkled her nose at the dropped apple core and took great pains to avoid it. She held her skirts up as if rats ran around her ankles.

Albert held back a laugh. He almost felt like a hero scooping the apple core over to the taxi tied at the curb. The draft horse dipped his massive head from the loose reins to nibble at it. "We were just admiring your window scene, Miss Dora."

"It's quite beautiful," Calista agreed. "I am amazed at how quickly you've been able to create so many adorable tea cozies. And the spinning snowflakes, my goodness, you've outdone yourself!"

Dora preened as she smoothed her skirt and coat back into place. "I do pride myself on quick work well done. I've been making tiny crocheted snowmen to add in the center tea party."

Albert watched the two women as Dora explained in detail how each piece was created. He couldn't help but see the sweet modesty and generosity in Calista as she complimented Dora's talent. Not once did Calista's voice take on a false note or draw attention to her own design ideas. Could she deliver as beautiful of a display? He hadn't had a chance to view anything by her hand. Albert wanted to see what she produced that much more.

The way she'd handled the boys, generosity seemed to be an ingrained trait. He counted back the days to when the notes were delivered. Nearly two weeks ago. Had she been bringing a basket of food to the street orphans every day since?

"Good luck, Dora. You're certainly off to a wonderful start," Calista said. "I'd better get to work on my display."

"Good luck to you. I'm sure you have something perfectly lovely planned as well." But the glimmer in her eyes said she didn't think so. "Though remember, you can't steal any of my ideas."

"Albert. Dora." She smiled and moved away from the millinery toward the Gold Block.

Albert caught Calista's elbow. "Do you mind if I walk with you a bit? I'm headed that direction for a meeting." *And I want to spend a few more minutes in your company.*

"Of course. I'd be delighted if you would." She took the offered elbow.

"Tell me something, if you will," Albert opened the topic. "Are you going to feed the newsies every day?"

"I really don't know. I'm doing the best I can with the resources available to me." She glanced up from under the wide brim of a winter bonnet. "As long as I have some spare food, I think I should give. Don't you?"

"What happens when you don't have enough to give? Won't they have become dependent on you?"

She strolled with her gaze on the ground. "I haven't thought that far. Should I not give when it's within my power? It seems I can only do what I can do. It seems if no one ever does anything, nothing changes." She lifted her gaze back onto Albert's face. "But perhaps that's where the Miss Snowflake Pageant can be beneficial."

"Feeding the newsies?"

"Not only that, but also bringing people together to see the children's problems. To open up a dialogue and solve the heartache of abandoned and orphaned children running in the streets without schooling or safe homes."

Albert put a hand over the top of hers. "I think you're onto something here. If the town's influential citizens somehow came together to provide for the children, it wouldn't rest so heavily on you and your parents."

"My parents?"

"Aren't they aware of your gracious charity?"

"Not really, no," she whispered. "I've been a bit on the discreet side."

He drew his brows together and his dark moustache twitched. "They don't know?"

Calista dropped her hand from his arm. "I had permission to give the apples, Mr. Shanahan, if that's what you're asking."

He caught her fingers. "No, I was only surprised. I have no right to question you like that."

"I'd appreciate your discretion on the matter."

"You have my word," he promised.

She scanned his face. Would this tall, handsome man prove trustworthy? He seemed earnest.

"What is that incredible aroma?" They walked a short distance further to find the door to the carriage open and Charles unloading the last basket.

Calista laughed with him. "Mr. Shanahan — Albert," she corrected. "We're constructing a downtown edible shopping village out of gingerbread."

"I'm going to have to leave you to your afternoon. I've a meeting upstairs. But I'm sure I'll be wishing I'd stayed here for one of your cookies! I do believe I understand the treasure those boys discovered."

Calista blushed, "Thank you for the lovely visit."

"The pleasure is all mine, Miss Calista." He tipped his hat and greeted Charles. "I leave her in your capable hands, good sir. Should one of those ginger treats ever find its way in my direction,

I'm sure it will have a fine reception." He winked and bounded up the stairs but somehow his heart's altitude lowered with each step he ascended. He turned and looked back as he reached the door.

Charles waited for Calista on the steps to the Gold Block. "I think I've died and gone to heaven with all that sweet smelling cargo all the way into town!"

Calista laughed.

Ginger and cinnamon. An aroma that shot to the top of Albert's favorites as it enveloped him.

ALBERT HEARD Calista's laugh float through the building as the elevator doors closed. Whether her display won or not, his heart warmed at the joy she spread wherever Calista Blythe visited. What would it be like to have a joy-filled home with a wife who loved to laugh?

The attendant offered him a seat on the brown leather benches. "Which floor, sir?" The stained glass windows threw rich rainbows around the car as the sun poured through them and reflected back in the mirrors. How could anyone think Helena, Montana was a podunk, an undeveloped frontier town?

"Third, please." He watched the ornately dressed elevator operator punch the black knob. They slowly ascended as colors played like a Montana sunset. Albert soaked in the beauty around him like he'd inhaled the intense spice scent of Calista's baking. Could this day be any better? Everything seemed to not only fall in place, but exceeded his expectations.

"Here we go, sir. Third floor." The operator slid the doors open and stepped out to allow Albert a respectful departure. He slipped back into the car. "Good day."

"Albert, my boy!" Mr. Power stuck out a strong hand. "We're all here and ready to get started."

Albert gripped the businessman's hand, "Mr. Power, glad to be working with you on this project."

"How are the ladies coming along?"

"They're pulling out all the stops." He flashed a grin. The men would soon be walking out past Calista's cookies on the first floor. If their mouths weren't drooling, he'd be shocked. "Gentlemen, thank you for coming."

Albert exchanged handshakes around the office. He took the seat left around the long oval table. The owners of each trolley line, Mr. Broadwater and Mr. Hauser, Mr. Power, and several other prominent businessmen waited to hear how the largest marketing endeavor Helena had ever attempted fared.

"We have thirty contestants busy designing displays in businesses up and down Main Street. One in this very building." He opened his briefcase and pulled out the fliers he'd had printed up. "Now our job is to get the word out and invite a prestigious list of judges. Here's a few posters for each of you about the Christmas Village Parade. The plan will be to have patrons touring the displays for two weeks. Anyone can drop a ballot in a box, but they have to go into the shop to do so. That means patrons are drawn into the stores. More potential for purchases."

"This all sounds well and good, but there are plenty of businesses left out." Mr. Broadwater said. "How are we going to include those businesses in this venture?"

"Sir, I fully understand not every establishment can take part. But this is our inaugural year. Surely those businesses not assigned a contestant will benefit from additional shoppers in the area."

"No, no." Mr. Hauser, the owner of one trolley line spoke, "I'm with Mr. Broadwater here. My business isn't gaining from this whole shebang. What do you plan to do about that problem?"

Albert sat back in his chair. Hauser and Broadwater agreed on something?

Another man broke in, "If the Hauser and Broadwater trolleys get some benefits, then my taxi service needs the same consideration." He glared at his competition.

Another added, "I just don't see how this is going to work. It's never been done before."

One more piped up, "My shop is not even on Main. How am I benefitting? If they get special attention, shouldn't I?"

Albert broke a sweat. This meeting was supposed to be a friendly gathering, not a barnyard posturing of roosters crowing over the top of one another. "Gentlemen, please. I'm sure we'll come up with some excellent solutions. If I could—"

"Well until you do, count me out!" Mr. Hauser pushed his chair back. "I won't be needing these." He slid the fliers back to the center of the table. A few other men followed suit.

Albert stood. "Gentlemen, if you'll hear me out—"

Mr. Broadwater pushed back his chair. "I merely asked a question. Aren't your trolley lines going to get business bringing the people in for the event, Hauser?"

A few grumbles sounded around the room. Most returned to their chairs. But not Mr. Hauser. He didn't leave, though.

Albert shot a grateful glance to the wildly successful entrepreneur. "What if we designed signs for the trolleys?"

"We already have signs." Hauser groused, "And those are a sure thing."

One man held up the flier. "Signs and more signs. It's getting to be a city of wallpaper anymore. The charm of Helena is her beauty. Plastering paper and signs all over tarnation isn't going to look attractive to tourists. You're going to have to do better than that, son."

"All right, would you give me a few days to come up with some more ideas? Something that'll be acceptable to as many as possible?"

"You think you're going to find a way to include the other stores that want to participate?" Mr. Power interjected, held everyone's attention as he paused in thought, and then nodded in Albert's direction. "Let's give him a chance, shall we? I, for one, have enjoyed seeing a few more people on Main Street each

day this last week. I'm putting my trust in Mr. Shanahan's ability
to broach this divide."

Albert took his mentor's lead, and asked, "Mr. Broadwater,
what do you think?"

"I think I'm sorry to have asked the question. But in light of
the development, I'm eager to reconvene and see what this
bright young man brings us. Two days, right here."

The men all shook hands, though the shake between Broadwater and Hauser appeared strained.

Mr. Power saw everyone out to the elevator. He waited and
rode down last with Albert. "Son, put yourself in the shoes of the
average businessman here in Helena. Ask yourself what you
need the most, what you want most, and what you're most
afraid of."

"I don't understand, Mr. Power."

"When you know those things, you'll know the motivators
for the store owners. What makes a man get up and repeat the
day? What risks does he face? What makes him feel most
successful?" Mr. Power patted him on the back of his shoulder.
"You think about those things and you'll find your solution."

"Uh, thank you?" Albert couldn't tell if he'd been given the
key to success or a quick trip down a deep well. But he still
didn't have his judges. They hadn't allowed him to get to the
reason the meeting had been called. Now what?

CHAPTER 14

*B*ut I helped make the cookies!" Lea huffed. "I wanna go see the parade."

Calista's heart clenched. "No." She wanted Lea to see the beautiful Christmas Village Parade as well. But it wasn't worth the risk. Showing up with a little girl in tow, no matter how differently she looked decked out in pretty clothes and clean as a whistle, it'd cause a stir. Lea would be in danger and so would the possibility of getting her to a safe home.

Lips pursed, Lea proclaimed with crossed arms, "It ain't fair."

"I know. I wish you could. But the most important thing is to keep you safe. Then we follow our plan to get you a new home." Could a six-year-old wrap her mind around adult logic? Probably not. "I tell you what. How about I bring you back a pretty collar for your kitty?"

"Ooo," Lea's eyes sparkled at the idea. "Then he'll really look sufficial."

Calista laughed and hugged her. "I think you mean, official."

"Official," Lea repeated.

"Let's check the ribbon he's wearing. I'll measure that for the right size."

Small boots clapped against the wooden floor as Lea ran back to her little safe room and returned with the puffy kitten. He'd already sprouted twice his size with the meat Lea shared off her plate every day.

"My, he's getting big."

Her little chest about popped the buttons off expanding with pleasure. "I take good care of him just like you said."

Calista held the black kitten in her lap, untied his bow, and measured it against a wrist. "I'll find the nicest one I can." She retied the blue ribbon. "All right, now play nice till Mr. Charles is back. Mrs. Brown will check on you shortly so I'll expect you to behave."

"We'll be having." Lea solemnly put her hand on her heart. Then she lifted Jesus Kitty and crossed a paw on his chest. "He says so too, Miss Calista."

A grin tickled around Calista's lips and finally burst forth flowering on her face. "You are the most adorable little thing I've ever seen. I do love you." She smiled into Lea's eyes as she adjusted the chocolate brown hair ribbon holding back her short blond hair.

Lea looked up from her task of making the kitten promise to behave. "I wish you were my new mommy. If'n you got hitched up, could you be my new mommy?"

Were they both in a fairyland? Hadn't the thought recently crossed her mind too? "Lea, if I had a husband, the first thing I'd do is ask him to help me be your mommy. But we both know you need a home faster than I could ever find a husband."

"Why? I sawed that one boy hug you." She absent-mindedly rubbed the long, black ears rhythmically like a tot would rub the corner of a blanket. The kitten had grown used to the gentle, slow circles and shoved his cheeks against Lea's palm for more affection.

"Because two people have to be in love." But Calista's mind quickly shifted to a vision of a blue-eyed, dark-haired young man with a close-cropped moustache. "And as far as I know, there isn't a fellow who loves me yet, either." For some reason, the vision of the dapper Albert Shanahan and his wide shoulders didn't go away.

Her fingers stopped rubbing fuzzy ears. "Oh." She set him down. Furry Jesus rubbed and wound between her ankles until a thread from Lea's tan and brown paisley pantaloons that peeped from below the matching paisley smock caught his attention. He flopped over, with his head on her bootlaces and tail swishing, and batted at it while trying to catch the string in his teeth. "Maybe the real Jesus can help. We're gonna go talk ta him 'bout it."

Lea spun and ran back to her room with the kitten fast on her trail chasing the flying string.

ALBERT HEAVED A SIGH OF RELIEF. The meeting ended in time for the festival ribbon cutting and parade to start. With the trolley competitors installed as judges and six of the prime off Main Street business owners, the judging panel was much larger than he'd planned. But that was a small concession to keep the pageant on track.

"Wise move, young man, wise move!" Mr. Power clapped Albert on the back. "Adding the them to your judging panel, and the finale at the Broadwater Hotel, works well for a larger crowd. Smart. But promoting the trolleys to bring the crowd and getting Broadwater to offer a special overnight package — a stunning work of marketing genius!"

Albert clasped the outstretched handshake. "I couldn't have done it without your advice, sir." He slid his notes back into the envelope and then into his briefcase. "With the size of the crowd, I think my ballroom would be too small anyway. But I can still house the ladies and their attendants the next two weeks as planned."

"How will you accommodate them on the day of the finale?"

"The Broadwater has set aside some rooms nearest the ballroom for the ladies to prepare. Then after the competition, they'll be able to stay overnight before catching the train or trolley the next day home."

"I do believe you've thought of everything."

"I've tried, but with every first there's always something missed." Albert buckled his case closed. With an offhand chuckle, he said, "I wonder what challenge I haven't foreseen."

"Don't jinx yourself, my boy." He walked Albert out of the office and closed the door. "Every challenge is just an opportunity to test your resourcefulness and your character."

CHAPTER 15

*S*tationed inside the large building with her gingerbread village display at the Gold Block, Calista's heart raced. She pulled off the draping cloth. The ginger scent wafted through the entire area, though the town made of sweets already ranged from several days old to the last gingerbread building she'd put in place on the hill.

The cookies would still be edible after the competition, if quite stale. But after two weeks, the exhibit would be covered in dust from the road every time the door opened blasting bad weather into the jewelry storefront.

What if people didn't come? What if people didn't think her idea had merit? Would it all be for naught? She straightened the cranberry velvet jacket embroidered in a diamond pattern of matching thread. Each diamond puffed and made the suit appear quilted. The puffed sleeves accented the tightly tailored waist and the A-line skirt flared elegantly around her. The mini-mized bustle style skimmed Calista's frame. She'd chosen the outfit for the sense of confidence it gave her.

The gold and pink lacquer rose watch pinned to her lapel read ten minutes to the ribbon cutting. "The ribbon cutting!" Calista bolted to the coat rack. She was at the north end of Main and needed to hightail it several blocks to the south end lickety-split. She cringed. A lady couldn't be seen racing down the sidewalk or arriving late.

She turned to the shop owners. "I'm so sorry. I don't mean to be rude," she explained as she buttoned up her matching coat. "I completely confused myself and should be at the opening ceremony for the festival first."

A moment later, on the sidewalk, she flagged down the yellow trolley and breathed a sigh of relief. The trolley squealed to a stop on the corner. Fishing a dime out of her reticule, Calista boarded for the three-minute ride.

ALL THE OTHER contestants had checked in well before the ceremony. They waited in the tent, out of the wicked breeze, behind the wooden platform. Only two steps up, Albert hadn't had the time to build a bigger one. Six-feet-by-six-feet, it could also be moved by a few men into position and back out of the street. Albert eyed the building dark clouds. He couldn't wait much longer for Calista Blythe.

The trolley pulled to a stop, rails screeching against the wheels. Calista alighted and hurried to the top of the street. "I'm so sorry. I confused my schedule."

Albert released the tension in his shoulders. "I'm glad you made it. We're just ready to start."

As Dora sidled over to Albert, the finely formed pleats of her black and white striped walking skirt rippled under the sumptuous black fur winter cape. "Shouldn't she be docked for tardiness?" Dora tipped her head and sweetened her voice, "I'm sure the courthouse clock chimed the hour. I thought the rules stated each contestant must be on time for all events. Is that true or do I possibly have it wrong?"

Albert set the rules. It was definitely true. He'd have to report any tardy contestant. "Miss Dora, we're using my pocket watch. I don't think we can count on the courthouse clock. It says something different on each side of the tower." As if in agreement, the clock tower bonged again. "We'll have to use mine due to the variety of events and places."

He flipped his pocket watch open. "Miss Dora, she's made it with a minute to spare." He looked at the two women. "But should a points question arise, the judges will determine it. I need to stay out of the decision to keep it a fair contest."

"Well then, if she made it." She shot a withering glare at Calista then flounced back to her spot behind the ribbon. "We all need to follow the same rules."

Closing the gold watchcase, Albert chanced a glance at Calista. Her stricken face sent a punch of compassion through his blood. She blushed deep scarlet, nearly matching her velvet ensemble. If only he could wrap Calista in his arms and soothe her humiliation. But instead he had to leave her to recover or appear biased. Would he be able to speak with her without the others assuming he could rig the outcome?

"Ladies and gentlemen, it is my great honor to introduce the Honorable Governor, Mr. Joseph Toole, of the great state of Montana." Albert paused for the applause. "He'll open our festival by cutting our ribbon." He paused for another round of jovial applause and then introduced the judges and the businesses they represented. Each man took a step forward, waved to handclapping around the stage, and stepped back into the line. Then the contestants had a momentary introduction with their names.

Prior to announcing the opening of the competition, Albert explained the fortnight of festivities leading up to the coronation ball and crowning. "The main event we're gathered for today is the Miss Snowflake interior design skills. Each of our lovely ladies expressed herself by creating a Christmas village in a storefront. She was allowed to use anything to do this and has been allowed two assistants, but she must have designed and implemented a Christmas village that represents something about the people of our great state of Montana."

The crowd roared at the reference to Montana's new statehood. It took several minutes for quiet to descend again.

Albert thanked everyone on the dais. "Our lovely ladies will then be taken by trolley, we have both of our prestigious Helena trolley companies have graciously brought a car, to each of their dioramas to answer your questions and help you find the voting box. Be sure to place your ballot. All points will be awarded during the finale on Christmas Eve, when we crown our very first Miss Snowflake!"

Albert directed the newsies he'd hired for the event to wander through the crowd handing out the program with the contestant names, corresponding store where each village display could be found, the name of each lady's village, and ballots. The boys dodged in and out and around the people spread through the street.

"Honorable sir, would you open our competition?"

Governor Toole stepped up to the ribbon. He stood at Albert's side and raised a hand to greet the crowd covering the street, sidewalk, and congregating in doorways.

The photographer, with his new push button Eastman Kodak camera stood far enough north of the staged ceremony to fit in the crowd, counted to three and snapped the pre-cutting photo.

Taking a deep breath, Albert projected his voice to the gathering. "Sir, would you do us the great honor of opening the Miss Snowflake Christmas Village Festival?" Albert held the large scissors while the governor grasped the other side. The two men posed with all thirty contestants arced in a semicircle to each side of the platform.

Again the photographer memorialized the moment.

Then he made the cut. The massive red ribbon dropped to the dirt. Everyone cheered. The photographer snapped away as fast as he could.

Albert scanned the many faces congratulating the pageant

contestants, pressing in to shake the governor's hand, and hailing friends. The downtown area, packed with people of all ages, struck a sense of elation that flowed like electricity. *It's a hit!* A slow smile of satisfaction spread across his face. This moment started the future — and he, Albert Shanahan, had a hand in the future success of Montana.

He sought one face. The one that mattered. The electricity flowing through the event zapped Albert as his gaze connected with Calista's. She trembled as if she felt it too. They must be the only two not moving an inch in all the chaos. What if she won? Could he wait a year before claiming her as his?

THE GOVERNOR'S presence raised the level of celebration and community pride. But Calista's attention wasn't on the governor.

Albert broke the magnetic bond. But his gaze flicked back to her several times. "Miss Snowflake contestants, please attend to your Christmas village displays. Ladies and gentlemen, we'll give the ladies a short time to reach their assigned areas. In the meantime, we offer you the opportunity to meet Governor Toole."

As Calista stepped out of the crowded staging area, Frankie saw her. "Miss Calista, Miss Calista!" He waved his arms. "Over here."

All the other newsies stopped and looked. "It's Miss Calista!" The boys excitedly raced to say hello, clamoring about her for attention.

The hair on the back of Calista's neck tingled as she became aware of every eye in the area focused on the sea of boys circling her. But she gave her time to the boys. It'd only take a minute to catch up on their day and make arrangements to share the biscuits when her exhibition ended.

"Boys, boys, boys —" A man's voice cut through their chatter. "You have a job to do."

Calista looked up into a smiling face, and then in a loud whisper to the boys said, "Remember, meet me at my carriage at five. Pass it around."

"We'll be there, Mith Calithta!" Joey piped up. He'd been holding her pinky finger, almost close to holding her hand, but not quite. He slipped his hand away. "Sorry, mith."

She bent down, "Joey, you can hold my hand any time."

He grinned.

"Why, where's your other tooth? Two gone now?" She tugged the brim of his cap and winked. "See you in a few hours. Now scoot and get finished."

The boys raced into the throng, grinning as they handed out the brochures. Stunned by the cheerfulness, festival attendees began smiling back.

"Somehow you alone have tamed the wild beasts of the streets." Albert gestured at one of the newsies shaking hands with Governor Toole. "Perhaps others will follow your example of kindness."

"It's more than that, Albert. I really care about those boys." Calista's eyes clouded. "I need to get to my display. If other people are going to care about the street children, someone has to tell them."

Admiration glowed in his eyes. "It isn't their fault. Being dumped at the last stop on the orphan train like you said, I wish there was something I could do."

"You're doing good things for them by hiring the newsies to run your messages and pass out the brochures. You, like me, can only do what you can do." She touched his arm. "But together, as a modern city, I know we can do more." She smiled, but removed her hand from his arm. "I'd better get down the street before people make it to the Gold Block before I do."

"You have time. Don't get frazzled." He held her gaze. "I'm looking forward to seeing your final display. It was covered today when I met there for the judging panel."

Calista's smile turned mysterious. "I know." Covering the

gingerbread village gave her the opportunity to keep the final reveal for a time she could be present to explain to visitors.

She strolled around the start of the window parade, waiting for the trolley departure and admiring the other Christmas villages in the windows nearest the podium. The four-story brick and stone Cosmopolitan Hotel's lovely glass front sat next to a stone arch doorway. It suited Millie Pembroke's fairy tale village theme. She created it around the newly published hit, The Blue Fairy Book, and even placed her copy on a photo easel, opened to the The Brave Little Tailor.

Thimbles for stools, pin cushions for tables, and card decks for beds. Millie used spools of white thread pulled off and pooled in piles to create a sense of snow spilled all over the ground. A cute little carved toy soldier became the tailor sporting a new handmade suit jacket with yellow cording around his neck like a measuring tape. He had a tiny blue belt, painted with white calligraphy, in a fine hand, "7 At 1 Blow".

Millie came out to see Calista. "Do you like it?"

"It's adorable. Wouldn't it be fun to be a child again?" Calista smiled as she thought of Lea climbing into the make-believe world. She'd have to remember to read some of the fairytales to Lea. "So creative and smart. Where did you find the soldiers and the horse?"

"My younger brother grew out of them last year. He thought it was great fun letting me have his old toys for this." Millie leaned over to whisper. "Dora is upset with me though. She says I shouldn't have used the sewing notions because they came from her store."

"I wouldn't give it a second thought. The rules said nothing about what to use or how it could be used. We simply had to create an imaginative Christmas village." Calista pointed at the real rocks, "And you even remembered the rocks he tricked the giants with by pelting them while they slept. But the giant bed made out of a cigar box is just perfect compared to the card deck!"

"There's the unicorn stuck in the tree." Millie showed her how she'd glued the wooden horse, head first, into an evergreen twig. "I don't care how the pageant turns out, I'm having a brilliant time creating something like this out of odds and ends no one wanted anymore. I think it would be fun to remake children's toys. Me, a toy maker." The ladies giggled over the boar made out of a painted thread spool and yarn.

Calista put an arm around her new friend, "I think with your precise painting skills and creativity, you're a very good toy maker."

"But what did you make? I tried to see it before the ceremony."

"Well, I used gingerbread cookies. You'll have to come by."

"I will. You must have been baking forever."

"It did take all the time we had to prepare, much like yours, I'm sure. But I'm happy with the result, as you should be of yours."

"What does your village represent?" A young couple, approaching to see her fairyland, interrupted Millie's curiosity.

"Tell me later. You better get on your way, it looks like folks are starting the window parade now."

A light snow started to sift from the slow moving clouds like icing sugar. Calista caught the trolley and sat near the front by an open window for the short ride back to the Gold Block. A glimpse of the miniature towns in Parchens Drug, the shoe store, the variety store, and the furniture store windows proved entertaining. She gave a smile and a wave to the competing designers as she passed each spot. Every young lady sat at a small chair and table set inside the stores facing the street view. Some had even decorated their tabletops to match the winter village scenes. Charming, and all so unique, like each pageant girl.

Calista arrived at the Gold Block along with the first visitors, St. Vincent's Cathedral pastor, Father Palladino, and Bishop John Brondel. They helped her lift the tablecloth and set it aside.

"I'll be," Father Palladino proclaimed. "My, my, look at all the gingerbread newsies on all the corners. Your affinity for that group of children is admirable. I can tell which buildings are which on your Main Street here. Well done, Miss Blythe!"

"Except that one near the South end. Is it new?" The bishop scratched his head, "I don't recognize it. Of course I don't make it to Helena that often. The town is growing so fast."

"That building hasn't been constructed yet. It's my vision for a future orphan home. She waited for the men, spiritual as they seemed, to laugh. What woman dabbled in city development? The suffragettes hadn't managed to secure the vote for women yet, let alone have female opinions respected in the male arena. But if someone didn't address the exponentially growing number of street children, Calista didn't want to see what would happen. She couldn't bear too see them out in the below freezing weather. How many would die for lack of a warm roof?

But the men didn't laugh. The bishop nodded, "All the beds are full at both the boys and the girls schools. Miss Blythe, we've outgrown the ability to house any more at the St. Aloysius Select School for Boys. We have no immediate solution."

A group of men and women brought a nippy gust in with them. "Mighty cold out there today," one man stated. "We chose to ride the trolley down and walk back up with the wind at our backs."

"Looks like we outsmarted the many people cramming in to see the first few windows," the other man added as he took off his top hat.

The couples wandered over to the heady scent of gingerbread buildings. "This looks good enough to eat! But it's so artful, it'd be a sin." Then when the man noticed the two priests, he crossed himself. "Pardon me, Father, and Your Eminence. I meant no disrespect."

Father Palladino's sense of humor kicked in, "Indeed, my son. Committing gluttony upon such a creation might cost you a doubled Hail Mary at confession." His eyes glimmered with mirth.

Everyone burst into laughter. Then the man's wife spoke, "What inspired you to portray the newsies? Their crisscrossed iced fedoras and scarves are a perfect finishing touch." She leaned in closer to examine a gingerbread newsie and his surroundings all created with fine tips and royal icing. "But what is that building?"

Calista knew she'd found a simple conversation starter and shared the plight of the orphaned newsies with the group. "I hope to see a safe home for all the children. But there's no room for them here." She gestured to the diorama as if it were the actual city. "This building represents my dream for Helena's future. A future where all the children are safe, warm, and cared for."

The priests echoed her concerns. Bishop Brondel promised to meet the newsies and determine a place of safety, warmth, and care for them.

Wouldn't it be wonderful if everyone she met that day asked not just what the building was, but also how could they help? "The boys have a hard time getting enough food and warm clothing right now."

Several more sidewalk shoppers crowded in as Calista spoke, Albert and a group of businessmen among them.

"What do you suggest we do?" Called out one of the men at the back of the crowd.

Calista smiled. She'd incited interest. "Sir, if each one of us did a small act. Bring a little extra food, offer a coat or a scarf or boots, or consider taking one of the boys, or even homeless girls, into your home. No one has to do everything. But if we all do something, we can make a difference." What if the boys found homes? Calista imagined all those young boys warm, safe, and with full tummies each night. It was possible. *God? Can you please help us help these children? And remember Lea's situation, if you'll be so kind.*

CHAPTER 16

The Miss Snowflake Pageant events quickly became a two week Snowflake Festival, with papers reporting on the success of each event leading up to the final celebration that would kick off Christmas season on Christmas Eve.

Albert took it all in with an immense sense of satisfaction. What if he could facilitate a festival like this every winter? The reporters from several newspapers around Montana shivered on the banks in shallow snow, but seemed to be about the business of interviewing contestants and snapping photos of the girls and the festivities. What better way to promote a Montana winter than through entertaining outings like this?

Society would eat up the sweetness of the scene whether European, Easterners, or the new Montanans. Many of the families joined the reverie. But the crowded skating park swelled with single men, twice the amount of bachelors than women. In a state with still so few women, searching for a bride topped the list for Montana's favorite hobby. The scales tipped in favor of females. The men worked hard to gain all the pretty girls' attention, competing with an impressive array of antics on the ice like peacocks fanning their tail feathers. After the pageant, there'd be twenty-nine single, available girls still. And the scrabble to snap them up.

A few enterprising boys warmed stones near the fire. For a pittance, they'd pull one or two out with sticks, roll them in old newspapers, and offer them for pocket warmers. Other vendors offered ciders, sweets, and nuts. The outing held the festive air that the Christmas Window Stroll had. Trains brought in outlying folks to do their big city holiday shopping. The displays caused more foot traffic in the downtown shops. The newsies seemed to be quite popular. Frankie had mentioned several ladies, while shopping, brought odds-and-ends to give away on the street.

Albert's eyes shone as he held out a hand. "Would you care to skate, Miss Calista?" The last few days dipped cold enough to freeze the pond over keeping the ice nice and thick. The pond wasn't deep or overly large, but it did bring people from all over the small city and it would be good for the Miss Snowflake pageant to represent the joy of winter recreation.

"I see," Calista pulled her mittened hands out of the muff that matched her burgundy velvet skating dress. She placed her beige wool-covered hand in his and let the muff dangle on its braided cord across her shoulder. "You're making the rounds on the ice skating pond as you would at a ball. Dance with all the debutantes? Is that the case, Mr. Shanahan?"

True, he'd invited many of the debutantes to skate. "You've noticed." He chuckled and looked fully into her face. The beige ruffles that matched the embroidered cuffs and wide trim of her burgundy coat fluttered against her neck. She didn't appear resentful or jealous not to be asked first. Calista's countenance calmly portrayed a sense of peace in her observations.

"Oh, pardon me. I wasn't trying to imply anything other than you're a superb host."

His heart warmed in the frigid air. He managed to cause her complexion to pink again by staring at her. But as they swept forward into the lanes of dancing skaters making their rounds of the nearly oblong pond in a waltz, Albert had a hard time focusing on the ice and not the feel of her body so close to his as his hand found the curve of her waist.

Was that all she thought of him? She admired his business skills and professed appreciation of his social skills. But would she come to care for him emotionally? Admiration and appreciation weren't enough. Albert realized he wanted nothing less than Miss Calista Blythe's whole heart.

Albert's blade caught on an uneven chunk of ice and sprayed the white stuff up on the ruffle at the bottom of her gown. He wobbled and fought to remain upright. In a smidgeon of a second, he released Calista and then toppled into a sprawl spinning on his backside.

Mirth erupted around them. First he joined the laughter and then Calista did. Albert's long legs couldn't get purchase — he was laughing too hard — until a few fellows hooked his arms to heave him upright. They helped brush him off as best they could.

"Hmm." Calista handed him back the hat one of the gentlemen retrieved for her. "Have I been the recipient of a special performance? I can't say I've quite recognized that new dance you just performed."

He loved her quick humor. "I do believe my dignity has been defiled." Albert swiped at his black coat, but the wet stuff clung. "But I owe you one more spin around the ballroom, milady." Albert bowed deeply, still caught up in the comedy, and brushed the ice crystals from the ruffle near Calista's feet. "Though I am egregiously wounded that you didn't applaud at a feat that has never yet been achieved until now."

"I do accept," Calista curtsied. She batted her eyelashes and then feigned a wide-eyed sympathy. "If only to allow you to regain your dignity, good sir."

He flourished the most dandified elbow he could muster to the giggles of those passing by.

Calista took it. "Perhaps, dear sir, we might simply promenade on the ice? I'm afraid another attempt at a waltz and we might both end up in a heap."

"I am but at your command, beautiful lady."

This time Calista didn't just pink at the compliment. She outright blushed red nearly matching her costume. Could it be that she might consider him attractive, too?

Albert perused the overabundance of men. He'd better keep an eye out or this lovely lady would be snatched right out of his hands. "Miss Calista, after the Christmas season is over, I wonder if I might—" A hand clapped on his shoulder.

"All right, Shanahan, you've had your turn skating with just about every young lady here." The burly fellow cut in. "Miss, may I have a turn around the pond?"

The ever-polite Calista smiled and said, "Thank you, I'd be delighted." She turned to Albert. "Mr. Shanahan, I enjoyed our skate."

"My pleasure." He gave an irritated glance to the intruder. "Perhaps we can finish that discussion another time." He handed her over to the new skate partner. His eyes narrowed as they skated across the rink.

A naturally perfect moment to suggest they begin to court after the pageant went up in smoke like the bonfire near the pond. How could he mention it before an intruder like that stole her away for life?

"Well I think you're spending an awful lot of time with one certain contestant, Mr. Shanahan." Dora's eyes bored into Albert's as he guided her to the side of the rink. "It might appear an unfair advantage, don't you think?"

They sat on the bench near the ice rink unlacing their skates. The small bonfire blazed a few yards away with a sprinkling of skaters warming hands. Light heat reached his back. But Albert didn't need the external heat as his blood started to simmer. Unfair?

"Miss Burdeen, I assure you again, I have nothing to do with the outcome of this pageant." How many times would he have to convince her? He tugged on a black shoe. The last thing he'd expect would be that anyone would consider Albert Shanahan unfair. And if anything was unfair, it might be the year he could be waiting should Calista win. The more time spent in her presence, the more he knew she held the hope for his future. Was it a betrayal to suddenly hope someone lost?

She challenged his explanation. "One could think that as you chose the judges and as the director guiding us in the events, that you might have influence in that part."

"I truly don't." Albert reached to untie the second skate. "I'm not collecting or counting the preliminary votes. The boys that deliver your messages will collect the boxes. Those will be delivered to the head judge for counting. I won't even see the final outcome until Christmas Eve with everyone else."

"You don't think people notice when you spend extra time with one of the contestants and not the others?" She plopped her fists on her hips.

He glanced up sideways from his position. Her dark blue woolen skate costume showed off her coloring and figure strikingly. But for a pretty woman, her vanity and demeanor left a lot of beauty to be desired. This was the second time since the Christmas Village Stroll that she'd pointed out a petty incident concerning the same contestant.

Albert sat up straight. Did Dora Burdeen see Calista Blythe as her most likely challenger for the title and crown? Or was he wearing his heart on his sleeve as easy to see as the ice patch on his rump?

CHAPTER 17

*C*alista practiced the music for the talent show on
Saturday. She had three days to master and memorize
this piece on her double-action pedal harp.

Tchaikovsky's *Dance of the Sugar Plum Fairy* would be lovely
… if she could concentrate on the fingerings. Calista leaned into
the instrument and pressed her cheek into the smooth, intricately
carved wood. Why couldn't she get her brain and her hands to
connect? The harp had been her favorite instrument to the
surprise of the sisters assigned to teach music at Saint Benedict's.
The thought of performing in public set her into a dither. But her
fingers stumbled on the strings as Calista plucked the chords for
this classical piece.

She could play *Away In A Manger* and set her mind on Lea's
face. Every night Calista, after she excused herself, tucked Lea in
and sang the Christmas song for Lea's lullaby. Lea knew the
sound of the notes and little by little found them with the fingerings Calista taught on the penny whistle. When everyone went
about their business in town and the house emptied, Calista and
Lea had spent hours learning the simple pipe so Lea could entertain herself. Calista plucked the strings on her harp and Lea

would match the tone on the penny whistle. Then she'd show her what it looked like on a piece of music.

The little girl picked up the instrument as if she'd been born with it in her hand. Music flowed easily for Lea. She continued to grow in confidence and beauty as nourishment and care wrapped her in love. Music was fast becoming a healthy expressive outlet for her.

Calista stopped playing as a pang flicked her heart. Regardless of the outcome, Lea would be gone in a few days. What would she do if the pageant winnings went to someone else? This was her chance to buy Lea's freedom and find her a new home. Without the money for the dead woman's debt... No, under no circumstances would she give Lea back to that monstrous man!

Help me find the right home for Lea soon, Lord. You feel so distant. Don't you know how Lea feels? Why are you taking so long to bring aid?

The harp rumbled under Calista's skilled fingers. The sweet little Christmas hymn had not likely been played as a battle cry before! Who better to cry out to in this war over a child's welfare than Jesus?

Lea tapped on the doorframe to the music room. "Can I play, too?" Jesus Kitty sat at her feet. He'd stretched out over the weeks and now his head reached Lea's knees. He licked a paw nonchalantly. The silly cat had full range of house and barn now though he most often chose to stay near Lea. Her mother and father hadn't seemed to catch on to the stowaway in the back room of the barn, but they'd given a grudging nod to a homegrown kitten.

The kitten turned out to be an excellent warning system. If the bell on the blue collar tinkled, Calista checked for the whereabouts of both her parents and Lea. Several near misses, but no accidental collisions as of yet. Though Mrs. Brown and Charles quickly intervened once or twice and scooted the two little critters out of potential discovery.

Calista pulled her skirt out of the way and then held out her arms. "Did you bring your penny whistle?"

Lea ran over and threw her arms around her new best friend. "I got it right here, Miss Calista." She showed her the thin pipe. "I been pracksing!"

"Prac-ti-cing," Calista touched her finger to the little button tip on Lea's nose.

Lea shook her head. "Uh uh. I been learnin' how to sing it, too. That's pracksing! Lots, too."

Calista threw back her head in laughter, curls bouncing. "I love that new word!"

"You been teaching me new words so I made up one to teach you."

"I think there should be an award for best new word of the year."

Lea beamed at her.

"Then let's hear how you're coming along. What shall we play?"

"I can do our song."

"Away In A Manger? You can do the whole thing now?"

"Uh huh." Her little voice raised as if the answer was a song itself. "Mr. Charles listened and said I was a the most perfectest penny whistler he'd done ever heard." She sang out the word *ever* as if it crossed the widest part of the Missouri River.

"That's high praise." Calista squeezed Lea's shoulders. "Then I simply must hear you play."

"I'm sorry, Mr. Shanahan, but the plans have changed. The contract for your event will have to be canceled. I've called Mr. Broadwater to meet with you." The Broadwater Hotel's concierge explained from behind the glowing polished wood front desk. A beautiful stained glass window drew in colorful light from the side of the check-in counter. "The natatorium has not been drained and we will not be able to hold the pageant in that area of our facility, unless of course swimming is part of the competition."

Canceled? "How is that possible?" Albert's stomach dropped into his shoes. He'd be ruined now that so much had been invested in this venture. The Broadwater as the finale host hadn't been chosen lightly. It became the venue because of the owner's documented statement in the newspapers. Guests arriving for the pageant would love the sumptuous surroundings. But without a grand ballroom for the crowning and coronation ball? Maybe he could find another ballroom, but how could he manage the myriad of events on the agenda with time so short? Three days! He had less than three days to completely revamp hosting sites and communicate those changes to competitors, investors, and attendees. Impossible!

Albert's mind raced as he took in the beauty of the enormous lobby. "Mr. Broadwater planned this weeks ago for the Governor's Inaugural Ball. I've built the entire finale around that setting."

The plan to move everyone to this resort area had been based on the higher volume of rooms needed during the last few days, the simplicity of everyone in one place, the variety of both performance and changing areas, and available spaces for services. Where would he put thirty debutantes, their families, and the judges at the last minute? Transferring them from multiple locations on a daily basis with trunks of dresses and sundries would be an outlandish task.

The concierge looked up behind Albert's shoulder. "Mr. Broadwater's here."

Albert turned. "Sir," he offered a handshake to the balding man. If he'd have been in a humorous mood, the glare from the new electric chandelier off Charles Broadwater's head and spectacles might be funny. He appeared as polished as the shining wood and glass around them.

"Mr. Shanahan," he reciprocated. "What brings you out on this blustery day?

"Sir, I believe we have a misunderstanding." If the natatorium and newly installed flooring wouldn't be available, then the largest ballroom wouldn't house the coronation ball. In this, he and Charles Broadwater agreed, tourism must grow in Montana. How could he not want the event that would bring hundreds, possibly thousands, to his new hotel? "Is there somewhere we all might speak and solve this difficulty?"

"Of course." He led the way across the red, gold, brown, and cream tiled lobby and up the carved staircase.

A few moments later, seated in Broadwater's opulent office of his suite, Albert explained the needs of the pageant. "With the public invited to the talent recitals and later the coronation ball, ticket sales of attendees, and the excellent reporting from our papers, I'm sure it will be quite a large event." He needed to maintain professionalism in the presence of this dynamic and successful businessman. It wouldn't do to make an enemy of one of the great developers and a Montana pioneer.

"I'll be frank with you." Mr. Broadwater offered a cigar as he spoke.

Albert declined with a shake of his head.

"I had every intention of throwing a grand ball for our governor and the people of the state of Montana." He set the humidor back down on the end of the most richly appointed desk Albert had ever seen. "Unfortunately, the democrats and republicans won't even sit in the same conference room to discuss matters of our state let alone show up to celebrate together. I'm afraid it just isn't practical for me. I'm extended enough with the grand opening of my grounds. You understand."

"I certainly understand the problem for the politicians. But don't you need business? How can hundreds of patrons be turned away? There must be a solution other than canceling the entire contract."

"Ah, I see we have caused you quite a bit of trouble. My apologies."

Albert acknowledged the apology with a grim smile. "I appreciate that, sir. But from Friday on, the debutantes and their helpers expected to be moving over to the Broadwater Hotel for the weekend. As you can see in the event planning contract, we have quite a few events happening here between the two concerts, teas, worship, and rehearsals."

He couldn't move the entire thing to another place with such short notice. How would he communicate it all fast enough? The papers couldn't be distributed in time even with the newsies help. Many of the attendees would be coming in by train from other areas of Montana and other states.

Albert laid out his plans for fifteen of the contestants to perform their talent on Friday and the other fifteen on Saturday. "It'll be a music festival and competition. I've already sent out the schedule based on the contract with the resort. Crowds will come for the entertainment."

"I believe there may be a possible solution, young man." Charles Broadwater adjusted his round lenses as he perused the itinerary. "I can't offer you the natatorium as the ballroom, but I certainly don't want to lose the business you've brought. I suggest using my establishment as your central location as planned, but hold the ball at an already established ballroom."

"Would the musical events, tea, and rooms still be available then?"

"They would." He looked at the event plans and back up at Albert. "Then may I suggest a new itinerary? My front desk could hand it out as guests check in for their rooms."

"That might work. Would it be possible to run a few extra trolleys into town if I can secure a ballroom?"

He smiled. "The Helena Electric Railway Company will be at your disposal for the weekend." Mr. Broadwater crossed out a few lines, wrote in the new agreement, and initialed the papers.

Then he handed the pen over to Albert. "Initial here and we have come to a compromise."

"I do understand." Albert breathed a sigh of relief and signed the changed contract. "I believe keeping it at the Broadwater will raise the clout of such an event."

"You've really managed to sell enough tickets?"

"Yes, I have a few hundred sold for the coronation and ball." Enough tickets to pay for the expenses and create a small nest egg for the Tomah Inn for the winter, and still there would be more sold at the door. "The recitals are also going bring in families. Though those tickets will be door sales, I've advertised them as family concerts."

"Then I'd better be ready, hadn't I?" Mr. Broadwater walked down the stairs with Albert as they talked. "Your ballroom is not large enough, I take it?"

"No. It can hold only about fifty. There are thirty contestants." Beautiful, and possible to hold lovely parties. But not for the size of a glamorous event like this.

"Have you thought of the Grandon Hotel?" They stopped near the entrance to the massive veranda. "The ballroom there should accommodate several hundred. Would that do it?"

"An excellent suggestion. I'll head on over there immediately." It wasn't going to hold thousands, but what if he'd over-estimated attendance?

Broadwater laughed. "And based on the meeting you held a few weeks ago, won't this just bring in more participation for businesses that felt left out? After all, the Grandon Hotel is not on Main Street."

Albert grinned. "You may be onto something."

He clasped hands with Albert. "Don't forget, we have the stables and carriage house. Plenty of room for alternate transportation."

"Thank you. I'll let you know shortly about the coronation and ball. We'll need those trolleys of yours plus all possible carriages. But if this works the way we expect it to, we're going to be very happy with the results."

"You have foresight and imagination, son." Mr. Broadwater added, "You're the right kind of man to take us into the next decade. I'm proud to be working with you."

Albert caught the trolley into town. Never had he considered the level of challenge over a dance floor. Or that the success of his marketing and publicity idea hinged on so many competitors in the hospitality industry being willing to work together. Now if the Grandon Hotel's ballroom were still available, he would pull off this massive event and they'd all be successful. But if it wasn't...

CHAPTER 18

*C*alista's harp stood ready in the Ladies Parlor of the Broadwater Hotel. She checked her golden silk and satin gown in the long mirror of her assigned guest room and adjusted the rosettes at each shoulder. Of all her evening gowns, this one made her feel the most beautiful.

The tight Victorian bodice nipped in at her waist, but still felt elegantly modest with two rows of tiny fringe made of pearls and crystals dyed the same light gold. One "V" fringe row accented her neckline and overlapped the next v-shaped row that dangled delicately to her waist. The solid gold satin over-skirt covered her small bustle and cascaded in a graceful water-fall to a short train. A heavily beaded A-line skirt ended in a pleated toe-kick ruffle with the same matching pearl and crystal fringe.

If only she could sell a gown like this to earn the money for Lea's release. Calista ran her hand down the soft, slick material. She loved this gown. She had other things she loved she could sell. *I love the dream of providing for Lea more than anything I own, Lord. I give you everything because you provided this all for me. Please use anything I have to provide for Lea. Anything.*

Was that even possible? Could she quietly sell a gown or two so Lea could go to safety?

Collecting her wrap, Calista smiled to her maid. "Thank you. I couldn't have prepared without you." The tiny pearl buttons that ran from the back of her neck down to the corseted waist line had to be done up by someone else. The maid had also done her hair upswept with bangs frizzled in the style most popular. Calista wore a matching pearl and crystal hair band. The updo would keep her long brown locks out of the way as she played tonight for the judges and audience.

"Glad to help, miss." She bobbed a curtsy. "You look beautiful."

"Thank you. I'm so nervous." She confided, "I've never liked performing in public."

"You? But you appear so confident."

"Appearances can be deceiving." Calista took a deep breath. "My heart is pounding so loud I think they can hear it in the lobby." The women shared a congenial laugh. The laughter sent a calm through Calista as she reached for the ornamental brass door handle. Another deep breath and she swept out the door to the top of the grand staircase.

ALBERT WAITED at the bottom stair near the glossy carved handrail. He'd climbed the stairs to guide each contestant down to line them up and then seat them in order of their scheduled performance. Singers, pianists, poets, all accomplished and talented debutantes trained to entertain at house parties and society events. Many Albert had watched in the last season or two as they were introduced to society.

However Calista's schooling away kept her talent unknown — like the light under a bushel. Tonight, he hoped her light would shine. That she'd chosen to play the harp intrigued him.

The grace in the hands and arms of harpists brought forth an entire symphony of sound. The instrument awed him.

Albert flipped open his pocket watch. She'd be expected any second as one of the last competitors. He looked up the stairs — and there she stood. The light from the chandeliers shimmered off her gown creating an ethereal glow that sparkled around her entire being. His heartbeat picked up speed as if a trolley ran out of control on a hill without brakes.

Calista saw Albert and rewarded him with a smile that slammed into his heart with an electric zap as if that trolley had just jumped the tracks.

His feet carried him to her with a mind of their own. "You cannot imagine how beautiful you are to me," Albert whispered.

"I—" Calista's hand fluttered to her heart.

"Are we walking in together then?" Dora approached the top of the staircase with her mother. Dora's yellow dress ruffled layer after layer. A large yellow butterfly made of matching silk rested on her right shoulder and a giant bouquet of pink, fuchsia, and ivory flowers set off by tiny green leaves topped the sleeve on her left shoulder. Embroidered butterflies and flowers the size of flagstones crawled up the sides of the gown. Dora looked as if she wore a garden, albeit a pretty one if one were wearing a garden.

Such similar colors, yet Dora paled in gaudiness next to the elegance of Calista. It wasn't so much the dresses the two women wore. Albert recognized the dignity and grace in Calista's comportment. She moved with a lithe loveliness.

As the host, Albert offered an arm to each young lady and escorted them down the grand staircase to their entry places. He went back for the last contestant, Mirielle.

The huge heavy pocket doors slid open and Albert ushered all the contestants to their seating section. Everyone, audience and judges, turned to applaud as he announced each name ending with Dora, Calista, and Mirielle. Skirts swished and swirled into the rows of plush leather chairs. Then he left them to introduce the second night series of the recital.

Dora chose to perform a sonnet. But rather than read the poetry, she'd memorized it. The dramatic delivery entranced a number of spectators. Vocal inflection, perfection in hanging pauses, and Dora projected her voice so well that the back of the room heard almost every word. Calista watched as the judges smiled, nodded, and applauded.

Head held high, Dora flourished a deep curtsy to the judges. Then to the audience. With a nimble ladylike twist of her gloved hand, palm toward her own face like she caressed an apple on the tree in the Garden of Eden, Dora gave a parade wave. Then she flounced off the dais as if she'd bested the serpent.

Calista closed her eyes. *Lord, I don't have that kind of confidence. Please help me to not embarrass myself. I'm willing to do anything to help Lea, but this is at the end of my abilities.*

Albert announced Calista as her harp wheeled in behind him by a staging assistant. "Miss Calista Blythe, our next contestant, hails from Helena also. She's an accomplished musician, speaks French in addition to English, and is our Gingerbread Village creator. She will perform tonight on the harp." He swept his arm out to invite her and stepped aside as Calista came slowly forward from the second row.

She acknowledged the judges and crowd with a flicker of a smile. Calista focused on her instrument, perched on the stool, and then took a moment to tune. She flashed a big smile across the room buying a little time to cover up that The Dance of the Sugar Plum Fairy had danced right out of her head — replaced by a cookie horse named Sugar Dance and the lullaby tune Lea had hummed. *What do I do, God?*

She spread her hands with pinkies extended out, plucked a string, and tapped a foot on a pedal changing the key. She'd do the only thing she could and play what did come to mind. Calista ran light calloused fingertips across the full harp as Lea's adorable face floated into her mind. The kitten. Their need for a loving home. *This moment isn't about me, and my fears, is it God?* Her ungloved arms ebbed and flowed in graceful arcs as she dipped her head into *Away in a Manger*.

Losing herself in the strains of music, she began to sing with all the hope in her that one little girl would have a permanent bed to lay her little head. The final arpeggio flew from the strings and hung in the air as if a cloud of angels hummed.

The audience sat mesmerized. As the notes faded, silence hung over the parlor. Calista leaned back from the harp pillar and turned to the audience. She blinked back a mist of tears as she returned from her musical worship. Her smile wasn't for the judges, but a silent prayer of thanks and joy. Somehow, Calista knew the Lord would provide. The peace in her heart flowed deep and wide.

The applause thundered around her as she dipped into a full curtsy. Albert held her gaze from the back aisle until she turned to walk back to her chair.

Mirielle Sheehan, a pretty auburn-haired Irish girl offered a lively jig next. Her feet flashed as she hopped and spun. It seemed Albert kept the most talented for last. But Calista clapped along, thoroughly enjoying the performance.

Albert thanked all the contestants as he moved up to the front then addressed the audience. "You've had a chance these last two days to enjoy the amazingly talented debutantes. Your votes will be calculated by an independent party for the top ten contestants, one of whom will continue on to become Miss Snowflake, our Montana winter tourism queen." Albert paused for a minute to allow the judges time. "Once done, please secure your votes in the envelope at your table." A rustle of applause and approval rippled through the room and then quieted. Paper and pencils rustled as votes were cast and stuffed into elegant envelopes.

He continued, "And those changes also concern the crowning and coronation ball. The Grandon Hotel has graciously agreed to host our pageant in their ballroom. We invite you to attend and find out who our lovely tourism representative will be. Please purchase your tickets at the front desk."

The judges sealed and signed the seals to further protect their votes. Albert directed helpers to collect the envelopes and deliver them to a local accountant for tabulating.

"Tomorrow morning, we'll worship together, and the ladies will have a Sabbath rest. Then Monday will be rehearsals. We'll announce the finalists on Christmas Eve prior to the ball, enjoy one final round of the talent competition, and crown our queen. Please come out and support the businesses and the contestants as we showcase the elegance and grace of Montana's culture."

As they left the parlor, Charles caught Calista near the door. "May I have a word?"

"Of course, Charles, what's the problem?"

With a lowered voice, Charles leaned in to whisper in her ear. "Our little barn critter hitched a ride again. Both she and the kitten are—" Suddenly he stopped and straightened.

Calista's parents joined them in the lobby. Their faces changed from elation to bewilderment as they spotted Charles.

Are where? Had Lea come here?

Calista's father asked, "Charles, what is going on?"

Heading off a scene, Calista controlled her rising panic and signaled Charles with her eyebrows. She turned with a smile, "Papa, Mama. Did you enjoy the concert?"

Mrs. Blythe effused, "Oh darling, what a beautiful choice!"

"Charles?" Mr. Blythe waited for his answer.

Calista placed her hand on her father's arm. "Thank you, Charles, I'll let you know when I know about the harp. I believe we'll rehearse here on Monday and then if I final, we'll need to take it to the Grandon Hotel next." She widened her eyes and wiggled her brows to show Charles she understood the problem. "Let me check for you on the transfer information for our," she paused to find the right word, "equipment. I'll find you to let you know."

"I can take care of that for you, dear," Mr. Blythe said.

"No, that's all right, Papa. I understand we have a tea on Sunday after worship. I'm sure they'll brief us after the tea. If not, I'll be sure to ask in time."

"Very good, Miss Calista." Charles stepped back with his hat in his hands. "I'll just be out in the carriage house." He quickly went out the door.

Now Calista knew for sure that Lea's stowaway talents brought her to the Broadwater Hotel. Charles would keep her warm and safe. But he couldn't get food to her from the kitchen. He couldn't take her back to the Blythe home without permission to leave.

What if someone found out about her now that she wasn't hidden in an unused back storage room? Calista had to get to the little girl as quickly as possible. Adventurous or not, the unfamiliar surroundings must be scary to her now it'd grown so dark out. Why hadn't she stayed home out of danger where Mrs. Brown could watch out for her?

The resort restaurant served a late night supper. "Shall we go into the dining room?" Calista asked her parents. "I'm feeling a bit hungry now that my nerves have settled."

Mrs. Blythe tucked her arm around Calista's waist. "I'm so proud of you. We simply must have a celebration."

Calista leaned her head against her mother's. "I haven't won. It's a little early to celebrate a crowning."

"I know how hard it was for you to perform in public, my darling one. But you did it! Not every success is winning a crown." Her mother's warm words hugged Calista. "Celebrate your personal success of facing a fear and overcoming it. That's a much bigger success."

She turned and hugged her mother. "Thank you, Mama." Would Charles be able to help Lea through her fears and keep her hidden with so many others around?

CHAPTER 19

Calista waited until she heard her parents' door close. She
changed into walking boots, and slipped a cloak over
her evening gown, then picked up her heavy reticule, and
quietly opened the door. Her blood raced as she did a fast check
of the hallway. Rows of long, decorative brass doorknobs but no
other guests at this late hour. She moved down the stairs as fast
as possible to avoid being spotted by dining stragglers or front
desk staff. With so many guests and employees, she'd have to be
doubly cautious. The pounding in her ears almost deafening,
Calista let out the breath she held slowly.

Once on the veranda, Calista glanced again around the
grounds through the darkness. The stables and carriage house
stood to the right around a circular path. She strolled the path as
if she couldn't sleep and needed a breath of crisp air. Lifting the
hood for warmth, her breath puffed in small clouds as she
neared the whitewashed outbuildings.

"Charles?" Calista called. "Are you out here?"

"Miss Calista!" Charles came from the interior. "I am glad to
see you. The little lass is a bit beside herself. I've kept her
bundled up and warm, but the kitten has been riled up with the
dogs on the property with some of the visiting folks."

"Did he run away?" The questions raced out of her mouth. "Did anyone see Lea? Is she okay?"

Charles looked up from under his cap. "Miss Calista, this has to end. That little girl must have a new home." He shook his head. "I know what we did was the right thing. But it's not right anymore to keep her hidden away all the time."

"Just a couple of more days." Calista lifted her reticule. "But let's make sure our little scamp gets something to eat tonight. And tomorrow, if you'll watch for me to take a stroll, I'll bring some breakfast somehow."

"What can we do to make enough money to get that little mite to safety? I'd put up what's left of my salary, but even with your allowance and my pittance there's not enough money to buy that contract off. Even if Mrs. Brown chipped in her cookie jar fund…"

"If I don't win the money, I have another plan," Calista confided. "I'm not sure how, but I have several things that will bring enough funds, if I can sell them."

A twig snapped. Both Charles and Calista turned to look for the cause.

"Did you hear that?" Calista asked. "Do you think someone is out here?" The breeze picked up and shivered through Calista's hair.

"My hearing's not so good no more, Miss Calista."

Calista strained to see in the dark. But nothing looked out of place among the shadows of bushes, trees, and fountains.

"Let's get inside. Miss Lea has been asking for you. Then I'll walk you back to the hotel so I'm sure you're safe."

She moved into open doorway of the building and down to the last stall as Charles directed her. "Is she awake?" Then she heard the little hums.

Lea cuddled the sleeping kitty inside the Blythe family carriage. "Miss Calista!" But she didn't crawl out of her blankets. Instead, Calista climbed in with her.

"If'n you'd hand me those couple of warming bricks, I'll go

stick 'em in the stove again. Been makin' rounds with them most of the night."

Calista handed the items to Charles and then wrapped the little girl and kitty tightly in her arms. "You scared me, Lea."

"I'm sorry. We just wanted to be where you was at." A bottom lip pudged out. "You ain't never been gone all night before. Who was gonna tuck me in and sing me our song?"

"I understand, but you remember why I'm doing this." Calista held Lea's gaze. "If we get caught with you before I pay for your contract, you're going to get taken away."

Lea's eyes filled with fear. "They won't get me. You won't let 'em."

How could both such fear and such confidence exist in one small body? "God willing, Lea, I'm doing everything within my power. But you have to know not everything is up to us."

Calista opened her reticule and pulled out a napkin filled with morsels from her dinner, Calista spread it out on the bench near Lea.

The kitten's ears perked up and his little nose wiggled at the scent of food. He struggled free of Lea's blankets and hopped onto her knees precariously balancing with whiskers close to the chicken pieces.

Calista handed a piece of buttered bread and a chunk of chicken first to Lea and then broke another piece of skinless chicken into pieces and held them in her palm for the furry guy. He wolfed them down and licked her palm to get every taste.

Charles returned with warmed bricks and tucked them around Lea. "I'll keep her safe tonight. But maybe you've forgotten something you need from home?"

Calista brightened. "I'm sure I have! Charles, you're a genius!"

Lea looked back and forth between the two. "I want my story. You forgot my story."

"Mr. Charles is going to drive you home." She took Lea's face between her hands, "And you're going to stay there while I go about finding a real mommy and daddy for you."

"You're my mommy."

Calista's face softened. She had to help Lea but couldn't keep her. No matter how badly she wanted to— "No, Lea. I wish I could be your mommy. That would be the most special thing to me. But we've been over this before. I can't be your mommy because I haven't found a daddy."

Charles left the carriage door open as he went to fetch the next brick. Calista heard his feet shuffling in the walkway. "All right, we're really going to need to keep this short. I have a maid waiting to be called to help me undress. It's going to look bad if she catches on I've been gone—"

"In here?" came Albert's voice. "Are you sure, Miss Dora? I don't see anyone."

"I'm sure I saw her come this way."

Lea jumped into Calista's lap, letting go of the kitten. He leaped across to the other seat and sat flicking his tail at the disturbance. Lea scrambled after him.

Calista scooped Lea back onto the seat and clapped her hand over Lea's lips. "Shh."

Albert and Dora? With her eyes, she communicated silence. How did Dora know? Had she been following her?

Dora's voice carried into the back stall. "What in the world would she need in here with that strange man?"

"You couldn't tell who he was?"

"No, not from the veranda. He looked like a dark shadow."

"But you heard something?"

"Yes, I heard them talking about money. She couldn't get enough money for something so she was going to sell some-thing." A short pause. "Do you think she's being, goodness, could she be getting blackmailed? Or worse!"

Albert's voice rumbled with common sense, "Let's not jump to conclusions." Another small pause. "There's the Blythe carriage. Maybe it was Charles, the Blythe family driver, you saw Miss Calista speaking with."

"I don't think so. I've seen her driver before."

Calista shook her head. Was Dora actually worried about her or trying to cast aspersions?

"I'll walk you back and then come search. I don't think you should be out in the cold like this. If anything is amiss, I don't want you to be in the middle of it."

"How kind of you to care for my safety." She simpered at Albert.

Footsteps retreated toward the main building.

Calista let go of Lea. "That was too close."

The little girl's eyes opened wide, as far as they'd stretch. "What if they come back?"

Charles returned. "Sorry, Miss Calista and Miss Lea. I felt it was better to stay out of the way rather than draw attention to you. I hope I did the right thing."

"Of course you did, Charles." She looked sadly at Lea. "But you must take her home now. Mr. Albert is going to be back any moment."

A throat cleared, "I'm here now." His stern voice sounded low, disappointed, and hard. "Perhaps you'd care to explain, Miss Blythe."

ALBERT GRIPPED the carriage door handle, more to calm himself than to block anyone from leaving. A dozen draft horses stampeded in his gut at the guilt Albert saw before him.

Calista's face whitened. She clasped a small, frightened child to her bosom.

Charles hung his head looking wholly defeated.

How could he let Calista compete for a title that represented all the refinement, elegance, and societal decency of Montana if she was of low repute? Worse, how had he missed untrustworthy character, and that she'd sneak out of the hotel? But if she were up to no good, using her manservant as an accomplice seemed both manipulative and exploitive.

Dora hadn't been lying. But Calista had. Was it possible his physical attraction to Calista blinded him and caused him to reverse the two women's character so badly? Albert's heart exploded in recognition of her deceit. This woman he'd laid his finances on the line for — he'd dreamed of building a family and a future with — was it all for naught?

Albert steadied the hammer of hooves pounding in his chest.

"Sir—" Charles began.

"I would prefer to hear from Miss Blythe, thank you." Albert stepped back to create a small path. "She will call for you when she is ready to go. Please wait near the door or in the warming room at the back."

Charles looked at the little girl, then at Calista with sad eyes. "Miss Calista?"

She closed her eyes. Then opened them as she handed a wrapped up Lea over to her driver. "Charles, kindly take Lea to the warming room."

He took the child in his arms and held her to him as if he protected her from Albert.

The little girl, bonnet askew, began to cry.

Calista picked up the kitty off the bench and set him on Lea's tummy. "These two could use a warmer spot than this."

"I don't wanna go." Lea's hands snaked out of the heavy blanket and wrapped around her lanky pet. "Miss Calista, I don't wanna go." Then she shivered in the cold night air that blew in the open doorways. She squished the cat until he howled with her.

Seeing the petite girl shiver and nearly strangle the black cat in fear, Albert's heart melted. "Is this the missing indentured girl everyone has been looking for the last several weeks?" He looked between Charles and Calista.

"Albert, I can explain." Calista put a hand on his as she

stooped to exit the carriage. "Charles do take Lea into the warming room before she terrifies Jesus."

Charles scooted out before another word could be said, with Lea sniffling in his hug.

"I hardly think a little girl's tears are going to cast fear into our Lord, do you?" Albert pinned Calista with his gaze.

Calista returned the confrontation with a laugh. "No, but the kitten is named after the Baby Jesus and I do think Lea might cause a bit of anxiety in that critter."

"She named a feline, Jesus?"

"It's hardly an unused name. It helped Lea to feel safe and like Jesus was really here with her in person. That He gave her a kitten when she had nothing else."

"Has she been with you all this time?"

Calista looked away. She said nothing, but lifted her chin.

"She has a home."

"One where she's beaten and that leads to a life of depravity!" Calista folded her arms. "That is not a home."

"How do you know?" Albert lifted an eyebrow. "Have you investigated? Have you talked with the authorities? Tell me, Miss Calista, what have you done to help the child other than aid and abet her running away?"

"I'll have you know I did investigate, Mr. Shanahan."

"Then you know she has a home. Why are you holding her and why here in the Broadwater's carriage house?" Albert's took her shoulders in his hands. "Please, Calista, tell me what's going on. I can't believe you'd risk such a thing as keeping a child illegally. What is going to happen to her now you've been discovered? Have you thought about the ramifications to both of you?"

Calista's face set like the battered stone on the downtown buildings. "What happens to me is of no consequence."

"What happens to you matters to me," Albert said softly as he cupped her chin.

She searched his face and then looked deep into Albert's eyes. "Did you know Lea's mother died?"

He shook his head without looking away, but Montana wasn't lawless any longer. Calista could really get into trouble. "That doesn't give you the right to act like a vigilante."

Calista's complexion flushed as her eyes narrowed. She shook off his hands and stepped back. "Did you know Chicago Joe considers that tiny little thing responsible for her mother's debts. Do you know how those debts are going to be worked off?"

"Be reasonable, Calista. I'm sure we can find a way to help her in a more appropriate manner." Albert tried to capture her hand, but she evaded him. "Calista!"

Planting her hands on her hips, Calista asked, "And just what is reasonable, Mr. Shanahan? She's barely six. At what age will the men of this civilized society begin to help that little girl pay off her debts? I'm not naïve. I know what's going to happen to an unprotected young girl."

"Let me try to help."

"While you're trying, she's going to get handed back to those … those … awful people. She's going to pay the price we can't even imagine because I don't have one hundred-and-two dollars for her contract." Tears fell from her blue eyes like torrents of turbulent rapids. "Tell me." Her chin jutted up again, "You want to help — how?"

Albert understood. This wasn't about deception or a misguided sense of kindness. Calista cared deeply how this small girl's future unfolded. She cared about the child's welfare as Christ cared. Calista hadn't acted out of vigilantism. But out of a deep desire to protect, provide, and love. Wasn't that what he wanted to do for his family? Protect, provide, and love them? "Tell me your plan."

"You're going to help me?" Calista rocked back onto her heels. Then she tipped her head sideways and studied Albert's face through pursed lips.

"You can't hide her forever. She needs a true family."

"Don't you think I know that?" Calista rolled her lips inward and chewed on the bottom one.

"I'm not arguing that fact. I'm agreeing."

"Agreeing." She gave him a deadpan stare.

He stared right back at her. "You joined the pageant. Why?" A look of dawning washed over his face. "And you came out to the Tomah Inn asking me to hire a young friend. Was it Lea?"

Her shoulders drooped. "Yes, but I know you can't."

"Not unless I buy her contract." Albert put his hands in his pockets and focused on the floor as he thought. "No matter how I look at it, I just don't have the funds to buy it."

"That's why I decided to compete, Albert." Calista pulled her cloak tighter around her as the wind picked up in the breezeway. "I have to win the money to buy her freedom."

"I see. And would you still be committed to the purpose of the pageant?"

"Of course. I signed the requirements. I will do everything possible to meet my commitments."

He nodded. "And the newsies?"

"Helping those boys will meet the expectations our businesses have for Miss Snowflake."

"I'm not arguing about that." He held up his hands to ward off a misunderstanding.

"Then what? Don't you think getting homeless children off the streets is going to help everyone?"

"I do, Calista, I absolutely do."

"Oh." She dropped her arms to her sides.

He took a deep breath. "I'm just wondering where I fit in, if at all."

Where he fit in? Calista's lips parted, but nothing came out. Her brain stumbled over the last several weeks. Images flitting in and out of walks, talks, and the exchange of thoughts until the memories clashed together in a jolt.

"Calista," Albert took her hand. "This is not how I wanted to ask. But I need to know before I fall any further in love with you."

She leaned forward, hanging on his every word, "You're—"

"In love with you. Yes." He drew Calista against his chest and circled his arms around her. "You have a lot of dreams. Is it possible you'd include courting me in them?"

"You want to court me after what you just heard?"

Albert tipped up her chin with three fingers. "I do."

She stared into the eyes she'd so often dreamt of and nodded in slow, jerky motions. "I do, too."

He bent and touched her lips with his. He lifted his head and said, "If you win, I will wait. And I want to help you find homes for the children you've come to love, including Lea."

"And if I don't?"

"Then we take that road together."

CHAPTER 20

Seated at the tea table, Calista leaned over to her parents. "No, I don't think they announce the finalists here, Mama."

Dora and her parents also sat at the large round table. Dora seemed to watch Calista's every move over the rim of her red lace china teacup.

"Don't they already know?" Her mother lifted a teacup, blew gently across the steaming liquid, and sipped.

"I think this is meant to be time for us to collect ourselves and have a Sabbath rest." One she desperately needed after sending Charles home so late with Lea last night. Mrs. Brown would tuck her into the cot and make sure she stayed this time.

"Sandwiches?" The server placed a green serving platter near Calista's father. "I'll bring another pot of tea?"

Mr. Blythe dug into the finger sandwiches revealing the Broadwater "B" on the china plate. "Did you sleep well? I thought I heard your door quite late last night, daughter." He passed the sandwiches to Mr. Burdeen.

Calista choked on her tea.

Dora opened her eyes wide. "I thought I saw someone

outside from my window." Her voice disingenuous, "Was that you?"

Gathering her wits, Calista said, "I was a bit over stimulated. I took a short walk on the veranda."

"Oh, I didn't see you there." Dora's face betrayed no hint of emotion.

Calista lifted a shoulder in a light shrug, "Oh, didn't you? I suppose it would be hard to see from your room." There, that should do it. Dora wasn't going to admit she'd also been out of her room unattended.

Mrs. Burdeen joined the conversation, "My, my. Calista, dear, one shouldn't walk about at night alone. Why it's just not proper even at such a safe, lovely resort as this one. One never knows…" Her eyebrows lifted to emphasize the unspoken inference.

"I'm sure you're correct, Mrs. Burdeen," Calista's mother agreed. "Darling, please don't do that again. I'd worry too much for you. One could stumble in that beautiful lake in the dark and never be heard from again."

Calista fought it, but the blush swooshed to her cheeks. For someone who didn't want to be the focus of dinner conversation, she managed to make herself the centerpiece. "I'd never want to worry you, Mama. I won't walk about the grounds alone again."

"I thought it was the veranda." Dora pounced.

Calista squeezed her hands together under the table. Had Dora been following her last night on purpose? Was it Christian to strangle a troublemaker? Probably not. "The veranda is part of the grounds. Thank you, Dora."

"Well, I'm sure your safety is all anyone is concerned about."

"I'm sure. Thank you for your concern." Calista squeezed her hands tight as she smiled. "Mama, Papa, would you care to swim with me this afternoon? I thought the natatorium's hot spring would be a lovely way to relax before the hubbub starts tomorrow. Did you bring swimming costumes?"

Dora looked stunned. "Aren't you going to practice in case

you're one of the ten finalists? I thought your session was set this afternoon."

Had Dora memorized her schedule, too, then? "I changed it, thank you." Watching from windows, knowing practice times — Dora seemed to have a bit too much invested in what Calista did or didn't do. It would be nice if Dora worried about Dora for a change. From now on she'd be much more discreet around Dora as well.

❅

"Mr. Shanahan, sir, me and the boys think yer gonna be right proud of our job." Frankie puffed out his chest.

Albert clapped the boy's shoulder. "Yes, I already am."

The Grandon Hotel's ballroom lit up with gorgeous electric chandeliers, not quite as large as the Broadwater's but plenteous. Rows and rows of seats held the avid audience who'd been entertained the last two weeks with the Miss Snowflake events leading up to the finale. Reds and greens of all shades, set off by white linens on the serving tables running the length of the hall, celebrated Christmas Eve. Confections and punchbowls sat strategically around the room for the intermission between the crowning and the coronation ball.

"And you'll all be waiting below to transition the chairs between the coronation and the ball?"

Frankie nodded. "Yep, I got 'em lined up askin' fer work. We won't let 'cha down."

Was he as determined as Frankie when he was a youngster? "The desk manager will let you all in out of the cold. He's a place near the fire for you boys. Any left-overs will be given to all of you as a special treat." He stuck out a hand.

Frankie grabbed it and pumped hard with the elation of a child anticipating Christmas... But then, Albert surmised the treats were likely his Christmas. The more he mingled with the newsies, the more Calista's passion ignited in his heart, too.

These boys, no longer invisible, mattered to Albert. He'd ask the chef to remove a treat or two from each tray. Tonight, the newsies would have a Christmas feast!

Albert surveyed the festive room and breathed a sigh of relief. With the hotel staff and quite a few of the older newsies hauling tables and chairs for a few pennies, he'd pulled it off. He smiled. Now the Grandon Hotel manager had access to boys with muscle for future events while those boys had one more way to earn an income. Maybe all this disturbance was meant to be for much larger purpose. *Almighty Lord, I don't know how you managed to make all these things come together, but I'm glad you're in control.*

Lights spilled out of the hotel as carriage after carriage unloaded women in gowns, jewels, and furs accompanied by men in formal attire at the Grandon Hotel entry. The battered stone of the hotel had been hewn out of the same quarry as many of the buildings in downtown Helena. The Miss Snowflake Coronation Ball held the fascination of people from miles around and held the prestige of top billing.

The audience and pageant contestants watched as Albert shook hands with the auditor and accepted the sealed envelope. "Ladies, the names in this envelope have proven themselves to be the truest of the true, creative beauties, and possibly the very first Miss Snowflake Montana who will represent our new state to the world."

Polite applause met his announcement. The young ladies sat to his right in a section specifically cordoned off for them in full view of the assembly. Three rows of beautiful women in elaborate gowns of green or red each dressed in finery with matching evening gloves and fluttering fans.

"You've all competed with such grace and dignity. There can

be none as qualified, as elegant, and eloquent as our Montana women."

Another round of approving applause with a few, "Here, here", tossed in.

As Albert tore open the envelope, it seemed the entire ballroom collectively sat forward on their seats. "Please welcome our ten finalists as they compete one last time. Once your name is called, come to the front. Then each young lady will be asked to perform for a final chance at the title."

The pageant contestants all linked hands and wished each other well.

Albert silently read down the list. What would he do if she won? Could he really hold back from publicly courting Calista for a year after he'd touched her lips? He'd already crossed the line by kissing her — and he wanted to do that a lot more. What if they were found to be involved in Lea's case? Would they lose everything or could Calista free Lea?

With a deep breath, he revealed the ten names in his hand. "Miss Millie Pembroke, Miss Dora Burdeen, Miss Alma Goss, Miss Justina Crookshanks, Miss Wanda Wharburton, Miss Rebecca Jones-Tews, Miss Mirielle Sheehan, Miss Susanna Farmington, Miss Delphina O'Connor," he paused and looked around the room. "… And Miss Calista Blythe."

Calista joined the other finalists at the designated spot in the front of the room. Most of the other contestants wore a shade of red with various embellishments from feathers to fur to pleats and ruffles. Her ivy green velvet with draped cap sleeves might have been too plain on another woman. But the refinement and flow of the gown gave her a sleek simplicity so she stood out like a regal swan among colorful parrots in their intricate designs.

She'd picked a ruby choker encircling her neck with two rows of scalloped diamonds draped against her décolletage. Teardrop-shaped ruby stones weighted the ends of each graceful garland, and the largest gem nestled against the hollow of Calista's throat.

The beauty of the piece brought light to her face. With her hair swept up and pinned with a matching ruby clasp, the gown became a canvas drawing attention to the woman rather than to the frock.

Albert wanted nothing more than to press his lips to the spot the ruby dangled. Instead, he gulped and forced himself to emcee. "Esteemed judges, ladies, and gentlemen," Albert swept an arm toward the contestants and backed to the side. "I am honored to present to you the finalists for our Miss Snowflake."

Flute, violin, voice, drama ... so many talented competitors. But Albert could only see one woman as her hands poised above the harp strings — and he hoped the judges didn't.

Calista lifted graceful arms...

As ALBERT WALKED BACK to the center of the stage, Dora leaned over to Calista, "My but that was a lovely performance."

"Thank you." Why the sudden compliment? "Your Shakespeare soliloquy was wonderful. You're quite talented at speaking. That will be an important asset to help promote tourism."

Albert explained the system to the audience and then asked the judges to finalize their scores.

"Yes." Dora smiled at Calista. "I believe speaking will be the majority of the requirements. You don't relish speaking in public, do you?"

There. Now she knew. It wasn't about compliments and kindness. Dora intended to undermine her confidence. She was doing a good job of it. Calista stared at her clasped hands in her lap. She wasn't the right person for the job even if she did need the money for Lea. Could she have lost Albert's trust and lost the competition so that she'd fail both of them? Albert promised to help. How could she drag him into this fiasco? But she'd used her allowance the last several weeks to provide the small things needed for a little girl — and a kitten.

"Calista, what exactly were you doing in the carriage house the other night?"

Calista's eyes grew wide and her face flushed hot.

Albert shook hands with the auditor and then took five envelopes from him. "I've just been handed the results of our judging panel. These contestants placed with the top five Christmas village entries, the top ten in performance talent, and displayed exceptional beauty and poise. Inside each envelope, this young lady has earned either the title of Snowflake Princess or will be our first Miss Snowflake queen. Ladies, will you please join me as your name is called."

Around her, the rest of the contestants inhaled expectantly. Calista let out a breath as slowly as possible. At least she didn't have to answer Dora.

He broke the seal and pulled out the first award card. "Miss Delphina O'Connor, congratulations, you are our first Snowflake Princess."

Delphina clapped in glee. "Oh I can't believe it. I didn't expect a thing!"

The audience giggled with her as Albert presented her with a pretty green mistletoe holly garland for her hair and an embroidered sash. Then he announced, "Miss Millie Pembroke, congratulations, you are a Snowflake Princess."

Millie surprised Calista with a hug and whispered in her ear. "I hope you're the queen." Then she whisked up to Albert to receive her princess wreath.

Albert opened the next labeled envelope, "Miss Mirielle Sheehan, congratulations, you are our next Snowflake Princess." Mirielle squealed and covered her lips with her fingers. Everyone laughed with her. Grins remained around the room as Mirielle dipped her tall, willowy figure for the ivy wreath and thanked the judges with a curtsy. Mirielle easily earned the most congenial of all the ladies, in Calista's opinion. She couldn't help but like her.

"All of our Snowflake Princesses will be called on for various events and duties as our queen's court through the year." He lifted the last two cards. "I hold two envelopes in my hand. One will be the first runner-up to our Miss Snowflake queen. She will need to be prepared to step into the queen's shoes should anything cause our queen not to be able to perform her duties."

The audience collectively sat forward and hushed. Calista looked around the packed room. She'd much rather have been sitting in the crowd than up here on the dais. Her mother waved and then she nodded as if sure Calista already won.

"Miss Dora Burdeen, you are our Snowflake Lady-in-Waiting."

Dora smiled and tipped her head to Calista, "I certainly hope you'll do the right thing if your name is called." She rose and walked to Albert while the applause held on longer for her achievement. A large group stood for Dora, including many of her family members. The ivy garland Albert laid on Dora's hair held a pretty pearl strand running through it along with the red berries designating her higher position.

"We have six lovely ladies left. For those who are not named, please let me tell you how magnificent your contribution and competition has been. We have had an incredible experience because of every one of your talents and personalities. Thank you to all of our thirty competitors. Let's give them a token of our appreciation." He led a round of applause.

"Now may I present your first ever Miss Snowflake, Calista Blythe!"

Did he say her name? The crowd erupted into a standing ovation thundering in Calista's head. A slight headache throbbed in her temples and her ears rang. But she didn't move.

Albert walked over to the line of chairs where she sat. He held out his palm as if asking for a dance.

Calista saw him, heard the crowd, and yet still couldn't decipher what had just happened.

"Calista?" He smiled, but it was clouded and questioning.

She placed her fingers on his palm and stood. "I won?"

He laughed as he led her forward. "Yes."

She could buy Lea's contract. She could help her get to a real home! Calista curtsied to thank the judges as the other women had. Albert placed the glittering snowflake tiara on her head. As she rose, Calista's smile froze meeting Dora's glare.

And one little girl burst into the ballroom with a bevy of boys bounding after her…

CHAOS ERUPTED THROUGH THE CROWD. Calista's head spun at the clamoring children, Lea's terrified cry, and all the confusion.

Albert dropped to his knees and captured Lea at the front of the room. As he lifted her into the air, a lanky black kitten erupted from her coat and clawed his way free of the commotion. Bright red claw marks marred Lea's neck. She cried out in pain.

The boys skidded to a stop behind Lea. But the kitten dove between legs and raced toward the exit.

"Miss Calista!" Lea yelled, "Jesus!"

The ladies gasped while the gentlemen gawked at the child's blasphemy.

Calista found her voice, "Close the doors, fast!"

One of the waiters leaped to obey and swung the door as the kitten slid into it headfirst. Stunned by the hard wood, the little animal crumpled like an accordion and fell over. He didn't rise.

Calista felt time halt and sound sucked from the room except Lea's horrified scream. The seconds hung in the air like fog as she turned to look at Lea.

Lea pushed against Albert's chest with a whimper followed by a gut-wrenching sob, "Jesus Kitty! No, Jesus Kitty!" She slid out of Albert's grasp and ran to the kitten.

Calista's chin arced slowly side-to-side as a tear traced her cheek. In a low whisper, to no one, she said, "No, oh no." She lifted her skirts and ran to Lea with people stepping out of her way.

Lea sobbed as she rubbed furry ears. "He's dead. He's dead."

Calista, not minding her dress, scooted in close and touched the furry ribs. Then she wrapped Lea in her arms and lifted her to a shoulder cuddling her close, but facing away from the tragedy. "Oh honey—"

Just then the kitten lifted his head.

"Lea," she whispered. "Lea, look."

The little girl's face morphed into astonished joy. "He's alive!"

The crowd behind them released a collective sigh.

Albert hunkered down and slid his hands around the kitten. Lifting him, he said. "Be very careful with him, Lea. But I think he's going to be all right."

Calista hadn't heard Albert follow her. But seeing him standing there with the injured kitten in his hands melted her heart. She knew in that moment she loved him.

Lea smiled through teary eyes and accepted the frightened feline. "That boy said he was gonna take Jesus Kitty and throw him in the creek." She tossed a disgruntled look over Calista's shoulder.

Both Calista and Albert turned around to find the culprit Lea accused. More women than Calista could count dabbed at their eyes. Men cleared their throats.

"That boy." Lea pointed.

A red-faced boy, about ten, took a look around the room and hung his head. Calista recognized Charlie from Frankie's group. "I'm sorry Miss Calista. I was just funnin'. Then she took off and ran up here. We was all just tryin' to stop her from interruptin' 'cause we didn't want to lose our jobs and treats." He kept his eyes on his worn out shoes. "I'm real sorry your kitty got hurt, Lea."

"Do you accept his apology, Lea?" Albert asked.

She gave the boy a long look. "I 'spose."

Charlie offered a shy smile, and asked, "Could I maybe pet your cat to let 'im know I'm sorry?"

Lea looked from Albert to Calista and then nodded back at her new friend.

The crowd murmured and a light smattering of applause accompanied nods.

"What in the world is going on?" Mr. Power boomed from the front row.

Lifting her head, Calista reached deep for composure. She carried Lea to the front, walking next to Albert, who held her elbow. She stopped to let Lea down near Charlie and gestured to Frankie to keep an eye out.

"Mr. Power," she acknowledged his question and waited for everyone to reseat themselves. "Friends," Calista cleared her throat. "I'm afraid I won't be able to accept this prestigious honor." She saw Dora rise and move to center stage. Of course, she'd be happy to step in. Calista took a deep breath. "I've been caring for this child since I found her shivering on the street. I believe the time has come to take care of matters that are outside my control."

Albert put warm hand in the small of Calista's back. "Go on, we'll work this out."

"I wanted to win Miss Snowflake in order to buy Lea's indenture contract with the prize money." A collective gasp encouraged her. People shook their heads. The evening seemed more like the recent melodrama Calista attended, hissing at the villain and cheering for the damsel in distress. Lea, it appeared, won the precious place of damsel in distress from the people of Helena. A lot of people, as Calista scanned the expressions before her.

Calista smiled, though it must look sad. "My parents told me I needed to return Lea to her owners." Her father's slow nod signaled her to continue. Calista's mother put a hand across her heart hugging her daughter from a distance. "But I couldn't do it. I feared for her safety. So I hid her — even from them. I'm sorry,

Mama and Papa." Their expressions oozed compassion and acceptance.

"I'm sorry to all of you, too. You have to know that I fully intended to be the best Miss Snowflake you could ever want. I just thought helping Lea and the street children was compatible. I hope you'll forgive me for the trouble I've caused. But as you can see, it's not going to be possible for me to carry out my duties." For a person who never wanted to speak in public, Calista delivered the longest speech in her entire life — and lived. At peace with her decision, Calista turned to Dora, lifted the dainty tiara, and offered it to the eager young woman.

Albert intercepted the tiara to Dora's surprise. "Ladies and gentlemen, I hope you'll find it in your hearts to admire the goodness in Miss Blythe's heart as I do. Perhaps she was made queen for such a time as this — in order to bring the plight of these orphans to light." He gave a warm smile. "Miss Burdeen, as the Snowflake Lady-in-Waiting, will you accept the duties and responsibilities of becoming the Snowflake queen?"

"I'd be delighted." She allowed Albert to remove the pearled wreath and replace it with the snowflake-designed tiara. He called Mirielle Sheehan forward and also replaced her wreath with the pearled one. The ladies beamed as the remaining two princesses were escorted to join them.

"Please welcome your new Miss Snowflake and her court." The crowd again applauded as the reporters took photos.

"Give us a few minutes to remove the center chairs and we'll transition into the coronation ball. Boys, you're already here…" He spread his hands to indicate the job before them.

The newsies and the hotel staff cleared the floor as soon as guests vacated their chairs. Waiters bustled about filling punch bowls and placing cakes, pies, and éclairs.

During the transition, Dora and Calista found themselves alone for a moment. "Congratulations, Dora. I know you'll do a good job."

"Thank you." She glanced at Lea sitting against the wall with the kitten cozied on her lap. "I want to help that little girl."

"I don't know what you could do. I have a lot of things to work out, but I think I'm out of time."

"I don't think so, Calista. I've chased this crown and forgot how important it is to be compassionate and loving. When I saw what you did with those urchins, and your willingness to sacrifice your crown and reputation for them, my own actions lately sickened me." Dora wrinkled up her nose.

Calista held out a welcoming hand. "Thank you."

Dora shook her head, setting her ringlets bouncing. "I'm making up for it. Will you let me give the prize money for the indenture? I don't need the money and I promise to sign the little girl over to you."

Calista shook her head quickly to clear her mind. "Did you say what I think you said?"

"I did. I'm offering restitution for my behavior and, hopefully, a better life for your little friend over there." Dora laughed and added, "and her fuzzy bumpkin."

Calista's parents stepped up to the ladies. Her father said, "We'll make that legal as soon as possible, shall we?" He handed Dora a business card. "Send any paperwork to me and it'll be taken care of gratis."

"I can't thank you enough!" Free, Lea would be free! Calista hugged her father and then Dora. She wanted nothing else than to share the joy with the man she loved.

CHAPTER 21

*C*hristmas Day.

Albert reentered the sitting room, after dropping off Dora's prize money for Lea's indenture paperwork, before Christmas dinner. Albert's dedication to procuring Lea's freedom immediately meant she'd be free as of tomorrow. Then what? How quickly would she have to give up half her heart?

"Calista, would you come for a walk with me?" The other half of her heart asked.

"What a delightful prospect, Albert. It's a lovely day." She accepted his hand and uncurled from playing with Lea on the floor. "I need to ask someone to watch after Lea."

Her father walked in behind Albert. "You two catch some fresh air. I'll stay and get better acquainted with our guest."

Lea, white skirts poofed about her like an upside down tulip, sat near the tree with toys brought down from a chest in the attic. She looked up, jangling a small bag at him, and asked, "Want to play jacks with me?"

Calista exchanged glances with her father. "Well, you offered." She laughed as he attempted to sit and fold his legs.

Albert helped Calista into her royal blue coat, though she left her muff behind, and guided her outside, holding hands.

"This is nice, being with you. Though I almost feel guilty." He pulled her hand through his elbow and kept his on top. "I think your father may have met his match in the game of jacks."

The late afternoon sun shimmered on the little bit of snow. Christmas Day. She'd mark this one as their first official courting date. One she'd never forget. He'd left his family festivities to make sure Lea's Christmas present would be the best of her life.

She flickered her lashes, "My father's out of practice playing with children. It'll be good for him."

They reached the end of the walkway. "He might welcome the chance to play with a house full of children." He stopped and leaned against the bricks that made up their fencing.

"I don't think I dare bring home more street children." She giggled. "I might just push him past his tolerance."

Albert caught both Calista's hands with his fingertips. "I'm not talking about street children, Calista. I'm talking about our children."

"Our—" Calista opened her eyes wide.

"This afternoon I did finalize the legal paperwork with your father for Lea's freedom. But I also asked for two more things."

"You, uh, you did?" The breeze picked up and tousled Albert's hair.

He pulled Calista close, into the circle of his arms. "Would you like to know what those two things are?"

Calista nodded, almost afraid to breathe and break the spell of those eyes staring into hers.

"First, I asked for proper adoption paperwork to be started."

"Thank you. I'm sure that's going to help when we find the right family for her." This man's heart didn't quit that he would think so far ahead.

"And then I asked for your hand in marriage."

"You did?" Her breath stuck in her throat.

"Calista Blythe, would you do me the honor of becoming my wife and the mother of our adopted child?"

Calista's knees gave way. Albert held her tight and pulled Calista in close to his chest.

"Does swooning mean you're happy about this or not?"

Reaching up, Calista slid her hand into the nape of his neck. Then she pulled his lips down to hers. If he had any doubt, she lifted her mouth from his and whispered, "Yes."

"Would you consider sooner rather than later? Say, Three Kings Day?"

"I would." And she closed her eyes for another kiss.

"Merry Christmas, Calista." He whispered into the delicate spot in front of her ear just before his lips touched it.

THREE KING'S DAY.

FRANKIE RAN over to Albert and Calista at the train platform. "Didja see? Miss Calista stole the headline on the Independent today!"

"Why? Because of our wedding?" she asked, putting an arm around the boy. "I can't imagine that a tiny ceremony would be headlines."

Albert pulled a few coins out of his pocket. "Here, Frankie, let me see."

"Me and Joey been selling more papers today than since I hollered, 'Montana now a state.'" He beamed at the newlyweds.

"What are you calling out for today's paper?" Calista asked after a glance at the front page in Albert's hands. Two headlines blared, one at the top, *Debutante Crowned Montana's Snowflake Tourism Queen,* with a small photo of Dora and her court. Then a much larger photo in the center with another headline, *Queen Gives Up Crown for Love* — Calista's shocked expression, caused by the children bursting in, and Albert next to her, dominated the two articles.

"Queen gives up crown for love," Frankie announced.

"Well, I think I made the right choice." She smiled up at her new husband.

He winked. "I do too." He bent down to kiss her. "Ready for our honeymoon?"

"Ew," Frankie grimaced. "When you comin' back, Miss Calista?"

She tousled his hair. "I have you boys all taken care of. Every day meet at our regular spot by the Gold Building. Miss Mirielle Sheehan and some of the other princesses will meet you with lots of goodies till I'm back." Placing her hand on his shoulder, she asked, "Would you boys let us help find you homes?"

"We'll see, Miss Calista. Them guys kind a like bein' free, ya' know." He added, "Gotta go. Got me some papers to sell." Frankie grinned and ran into the waiting passengers waving a paper high. "Queen gives up crown for love!" Within seconds he'd sold several papers.

Albert assured her, "You've reached a lot of hearts on those boys' behalf. It's going to affect generations to come."

"I hope so." She nodded. "But it's not over yet until the newsies and the orphans have safe homes. I have my gold, frankincense, and myrrh. But those children still have only a manger for their beds. I want to do so much for them."

"I know, Mrs. Shanahan, but this time we're doing it together." Albert wrapped his arms around Calista.

"Together." She sighed her agreement into his strong chest.

And the train whistle blew the opening note of their new life. "All aboard!"

SONG OF THE ROCKIES

BOOK 2 — QUEEN OF THE ROCKIES SERIES

Helena, Montana
   Winter, 1890

Mirielle spun from the schoolroom door. "What do you mean you'll send them to military school or indenture them?" As cold as the Montana winter wind blew against the new glass windows, the heat in her blood boiled. "The newsies don't need slavery. And they certainly don't deserve the misery of military life when they haven't even had a childhood!"

"Miss Sheehan," the superintendent spoke softly. "All the town council asks is for you to help round up the boys. You're not going to —"

"Betray them?" Mirielle balled her hands at her sides. "Those boys work hard. They trust me."

He sighed. "Those boys are going to freeze to death if they don't land in more trouble first."

"They've been fine in the Shanahan stables. Albert and Calista have created spaces with cots in the stalls. I want a better home for each of them, we all do. But they outright refuse. At least they're warm and safe."

"You made my point for me, warm or not. Refusal to meet the

norm means those boys can't fit into society. They're an unruly bunch and uncivilized. That madhouse they created during the Miss Snowflake Pageant was just the beginning. Running amuck like that in a ballroom."

"They were just trying to catch the kitten when —"

"It all worked out that time, but cat or no cat, it just can't continue." He swiped a handkerchief against his brow.

"Remember those boys set up the ballroom in the first place. That has to say something for their character. Store owners are hiring them for message boys and—"

"They must become productive citizens."

Mirielle shivered. Cold, yes, but confrontation always brought out a sweat in her superior.

His eyes softened, "As industrious as the newsies are at getting odd jobs to supplement their newspaper sales, the lot of them aren't going to make it as adults without some form of discipline and an education."

"Of course. That's why Calista and I've been meeting the boys with food each day and reading lessons twice a week." What did these people think — eleven young street boys would miraculously become model citizens? They needed love and people to teach them manners, not some convenient solution to rid the streets of orphans. "For pity's sake, these are the same boys no one adopted from the Orphan Train—to rid cities back East of miscreants. All well meant then too. Meant to rid them of a problem and dump it on other people."

"Truly, I'm not here to argue." Mr. Randolph straightened his back and dabbed his neck. "Either you help the merchants manage the mayhem or the sheriff will."

"You'd do that?" Mirielle shook her head as her eyes misted. "After all our work gaining their trust and friendship, isn't the goal to help those boys become solid citizens? They'll be like caged animals. Education is the answer, not punishment."

"Miss Sheehan, they're already lacking social manners. Most folks feel the newsies are living like animals. It hurts hearts to see children scavenging like that little Joey boy even if he does have the leader for a brother." Mr. Randolph rolled back onto his heels. "Frankie is barely old enough to be on his own, if he's truthful about his age. How is it right that he's trying to provide for a six-year old?"

She closed her eyes. "Of course it isn't." Mirielle opened her eyes and plead, "Can't you see separating them would devastate not only those boys, but shatter the group? Frankie has managed to keep a ragtag bunch productive. They deserve a chance with our help."

"I think they're out of chances after that last incident." He shook his head. "Boys can't be running amuck in and out of stores and hopping trollies like leap frog. Poor Mrs. Broadwater nearly lost her shopping bags and her wits when one of those boys landed in her lap the other day."

Mirielle almost laughed, but caught herself. The inconsistent trolley schedule irritated workers already. They'd be further annoyed by boys playing pranks, fun-loving or not. "Please ask the council for a little more time to educate them."

She looked around the room as Mr. Randolph deliberated. Education. Yes! Why couldn't the newsies come here? "I'll talk to the priests and the school board about getting the newsies into a classroom."

"I can't see how that would work."

"The church believes in charity. What better place for young boys to learn discipline and the social graces than an exclusive boys' school?" But how would they manage eleven new students? Even a church has limits to their resources.

"Excuse me."

Mirielle and Mr. Randolph startled at the baritone voice.

The intruder cleared his throat and looked at Mr. Randolph. "I apologize for interrupting, but I understand you're the one to talk to about some boys placed here as boarders."

Mirielle stepped back, the attractive man ducked to get into her classroom. She wasn't a short woman. But goodness was he a tall man — with sand-colored straight hair and light blue eyes and… She swallowed back a gasp at the sight of his strong physique. What in the world? She'd seen attractive men before. Mirielle puckered her brows at the heat searing into her cheeks despite her efforts to quell it. What a goose reacting like that!

"Miss Sheehan, I'll expect an answer by end of the week. The boys are in school and settled," he held up his hand to ward off her interruption, "or they're shipped off for a more disciplined education."

Three days. She had three days to convince Frankie to convince ten other boys to start going to school. She already knew the argument. How would they earn enough income if they sat in a schoolroom all day? But they wouldn't have to scrounge for meals if they'd agree to boarding school. It was all-inclusive.

Mirielle swallowed a groan. Where would she get the additional funds to convince the priests and the head master the new school could support eleven more boarding students?

Mr. Randolph turned to the visitor. "And you, sir, are?"

The handsome man extended a hand to the school's headmaster. "Evan Russell, sir." They shook. His eyes flicked up to Mirielle's as he also offered a polite handshake to her. "Ma'am."

A tingle raced from fingertip to elbow to shoulder to heart. Mirielle's eyes grew wide at the ripple. She couldn't look away from his similarly stunned eyes. And that ripple hadn't stopped racing through her arm like a sudden flash flood rushing into her heart.

"Miss Sheehan?" Mr. Randolph broke into her silence. "I believe your duties call."

"Um, yes." She snatched her hand back. Flustered? The teacher who could manage the toughest child and go toe-to-toe with the most demanding parent? She never flustered. What did he do to her? "My—uh—pleasure to meet you, Mr. Russell." Mirielle forced herself to back away.

His gaze stayed connected to hers as Mirielle bumped into

her desk and then felt her way around it like a miner in a blackout. A flush rushed boot to root. She jerked her chin away and plopped into her seat. Better to concentrate on grading than on being graded by strange man. She swallowed. Such a man, for certain, with strong, wide shoulders filling out the heavy wool coat.

He seemed to hear Mirielle's thoughts as his gaze still heating her skin. Electricity passed between them as strong as the gusts against the glass.

Evan yanked his attention back to the superintendent. Mining had been a long, lonely process as he'd built up savings to provide for his son and their future. He'd come looking for Joseph, not a new wife. But even his poignant memories of pretty Nadine didn't rival this russet-haired beauty that seemed to flush at the slightest glance. If he intimidated the little school marm, how in the world did she manage a classroom of children?

"Mr. Russell?" The superintendent waited.

"I'm sorry." He mumbled to the tubby man. "I think I left my manners in the mine." It'd been a long time since he'd experienced a woman's scent, er, presence.

"Well, how can we help you then?"

"My son is missing, sir." Miss Sheehan's inhale caught Evan off guard. He cleared his throat. It still hurt every time he had to repeat it, but sympathy choked him to silence. Do-gooders needed to either help him or stay out of it. He dredged deep for the courage to tell it one more time. "I left him with relatives after my wife died. I had to work elsewhere. For a long time, I'd get an update once a month. But those updates stopped coming a year ago. Being the dead of winter, I assumed mail was having trouble getting through. After the melt, I came over the mountains. When I inquired, I heard…" He ran a hand through his hair. "My brother's home burned down, and according to all accounts, my family was lost."

"Oh Mr. Russell, I am so sorry." Mirielle crossed herself and bowed her head.

Evan cleared his throat again. "My son was not found among the ruins. I was directed here to ask if any families might have taken him in and registered Joseph with their children."

"Joseph, you say?" Mr. Randolph scratched his head. "We have several by that name, but all have known parents."

Evan's heart sank. Maybe it was true. Maybe Joseph didn't make it through the fire. "Is there a way to question the children? Or let me see them? Maybe one of the boys was taken in or adopted." He knew desperation tinged every word. What else could he do? Where could a little boy wander off to without anyone noticing?

"I realize the dire nature of the situation, Mr. Russell. But there's no possible way we could impose on the families of this school for a search. You're simply asking too much. We know each child here. What would you do if he were found adopted? You certainly couldn't suddenly show up and abscond with a child."

Abscond? "Not just a child, sir. My son!"

The young lady cleared her throat. "May I?" Miss Sheehan certainly didn't wait to be invited as she offered, "What if the child weren't here, but a child here knew of him?"

Hope lit in Evan's heart. He'd have made friends. Of course!

"I do see all the children through music class each week." She rejoined the men. "If Joseph attended our school, I'd know. But, no sir, all of the boys belong naturally to their parents."

The hope dimmed.

"Mr. Russell, we could send out notices to the parents. Then if one of the families knows your son, they'll let us know. But I have another idea for you."

Evan's emotions jerked up and down like the backside of a bronco. "I'm listening."

"As am I, Miss Sheehan." The superintendent raised his eyebrows.

"Come with me to meet the newsies."

"The newsies?"

She held up a forefinger and tipped her head forward as if conducting an orchestra. "I know eleven little boys who would love to earn a penny or two." Her hands gracefully lowered.

The fatigue of frustration set an edge in his voice. " What makes you think a bunch of—" Evan clamped his mouth shut at the sudden fire in her eyes as Mirielle's hands pinched the air punctuating the sign for a dramatic rest.

She gave him a direct challenge, "Do you have a better idea? They can spread out and look in places no adult would think of searching. One might think your love of a few pennies—"

"No, no. Nothing like that." Now he knew how she managed a classroom full of boys. Could a motley cluster of newsboys fan out and find Joseph in Helena?

"You won't know until you try." She looked him straight in the eye, not a hint of falsehood in her voice. "And they're nice boys."

The superintendent added, "They are nice, if a bit unruly. But we have plans to solve that issue."

The teacher's back stiffened. "In the most loving way possible for their future success."

Miss Sheehan's voice softened as she placed fingertips on his bicep. "Are you willing to try?"

The weight of her touch soothed him even through the heavy wool of his coat. Evan nodded and concentrated on the hope she offered. He liked her optimism. Something sorely lacking in him right now. "I'll try anything."

❇

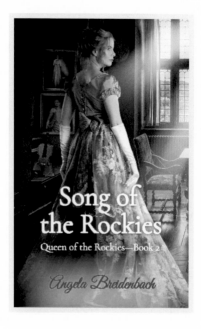

Did you like the excerpt from **Song of the Rockies**? It's available by going to AngelaBreidenbach.com or your favorite bookstore in person or online.

Look for *Heart of the Rockies, Flower of the Rockies, Bride of the Rockies,* and *Flame of the Rockies* to complete your *Queen of the Rockies Series* 6-book collection.

TRAVEL TIPS FOR HELENA, MONTANA

September. The magical month of the year in Montana that we don't tend to mention. A local secret. The temperature is perfect during the day, slightly chilly at night and in the morning, and the state turns a glowing golden. September is my favorite month of the year in Montana, up to October 15th to be technical.

Beyond hunting, fishing, hiking, biking, horseback riding, photography, white water rafting, tubing down the river, camping, dude ranching, boating, famous national parks and state parks... I feel like I should be saying, "Wait, there's more!" People not from Montana don't know how much culture our state offers. From festivals, art shows, musicals, plays, sports, concerts, and the food is incredible. You can visit ghost towns, gold mines, follow historic trails like the Lewis and Clark, explore giant cave systems (like the Lewis and Clark Caves — we're kind of proud of those guys and their team including Sacajawea), pow wows, rodeos, fairs, farmers markets, specialized sports camps, and your mom. (Okay, that last one was for my out-of-state kids, but you get the picture. Family is still big in Montana.)

Though I've been asked about the Wild West when I travel, Montana has a high level of sophistication along with incredible wild views of vast mountain ranges and plains. As I write this travel guide, the speed limit is 80 mph on the highway while towns and cities have slower speeds. Don't miss the 25-35 mph signs in small towns or you'll definitely earn a speeding ticket. Long drives are normal to Montanans. But we don't mind because the passing landscape is stunning.

To visit Helena, though, you'll enjoy some summer only activities if you come during tourist season. The train tour through Last Chance Gulch usually runs May 1st and up to September 15th.

Great links to plan your trip are:

- HelenaMT.com
- Last Chance Tours: LCtours.com/take-a-tour-aboard-helenas-last-chance-tour-train/
- Montana Historical Society (where I also enjoyed researching some of this story's history) mhs.mt.gov/museum/
- VisitMT.com lots online, but also guidebooks available.

Dear Reader,

I hope you enjoyed *Queen of the Rockies*, book 1 in the Queen of the Rockies Series. I had so much fun with Calista, Albert, Lea, and Jesus Kitty that it was hard to let them go. Then add all the newsies to the mix. I didn't want to say goodbye to historic Helena, Montana. I wrote another story that tells what happens to Frankie and Joey in 1890, after the end of *Queen of the Rockies*... I just can't leave them, or you, hanging... Will Mirielle Sheehan's love find homes for orphaned newsies? What happens when one little boy isn't like the others? Who is his father? Find out in *Song of the Rockies*.

As an author, I love feedback. Candidly, you're the reason I explored both the newsies and Mirielle Sheehan into the next book and the rest of the series. So, tell me what you liked or loved, what questions or thoughts *Queen of the Rockies* brought to mind, or what made you laugh and cry.

Visit me on the web at: AngelaBreidenbach.com or on the *Genealogy Publishing Coach* show where we discuss tips to discover your own ancestral stories. If you have questions or comments, click on the contact page on my website and send me a personal note. It comes right to me.

Finally, if you're so inclined, I'd appreciate a review of this story. Your feedback is important to me! Reviews can be hard to come by. You, the reader, have the power now to make or break a book. If you do leave a review, thank you! If you share it on social media and tag me @AngBreidenbach, I'll do my best to share it. If you review or interview authors on your blog, contact me. I'll be sure to share a review of my book or interview with you through my social media.

My newsletter is on my website, where you can also find more of my books at AngelaBreidenbach.com. You'll get an email only when I have a new release or something fun, helpful, or fascinating to share. Reviews on Goodreads or other bookstores are also highly prized. Thank you so much for reading *Queen of the Rockies* and for spending time with me.

Appreciatively,
Angela Breidenbach

MEET ANGELA BREIDENBACH

Angela Breidenbach is a professional genealogist with specialties in English Records, Scotland, and Lecturing. She's also a multiple ECPA and Amazon best-selling author, media personality, and screenwriter. Angela writes family-friendly historical novels steeped in local flavor, lively characters, adventure, romance, and genealogy. She's the president of the Christian Authors Network, member of the Daughters of the American Revolution, CIPA, ALLi, and FHL-CW. Angie lives in Montana with her hubby and Muse, a trained fe-lion, who shakes hands, rolls over, and jumps through a hoop. Surprisingly, Angie can also which comes in handy when wrangling any of her nine grandchildren. Don't miss her new show, Genealogy Publishing Coach with a grand opening along with a 6-book series, *Queen of the Rockies,* set during Montana's birth as a state!

AngelaBreidenbach.com

Social Media: @AngBreidenbach

New 6-book series coming 2021: Queen of the Rockies

Book 1 — September 2021, Queen of the Rockies.

Book 2 — October 2021, Song of the Rockies

Book 3 — November 2021, Heart of the Rockies

Book 4 — December 2021, Flower of the Rockies

Book 5 — January 2022, Bride of the Rockies

Book 6 — February 2022, Flame of the Rockies

Enjoy *Historically Speaking Newsletter* with updates on novels, nonfiction, and genealogy tips and/or *An A-Muse-ing Newsletter* with humor from Muse and Writer. Both will share events and features pertaining to their topics. Sign up for your choice or both at:

https://landing.mailerlite.com/webforms/landing/n0s2t2
or by using this QR code.

Tune in to Angela Breidenbach's podcast, Genealogy Publishing Coach on your favorite podcast listening app.

Romantic fiction: Historical

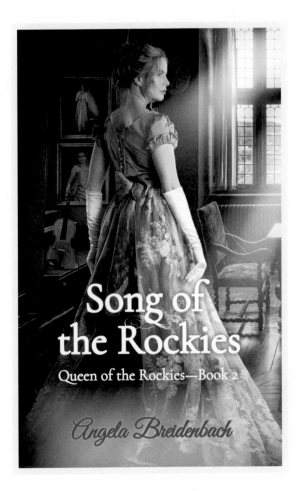

Song of the Rockies: What would you do with eleven rowdy street newsies, leftovers from the Orphan Train? Could you turn them into model citizens before they get sold into indenture or sent off to the military? What if one man showed up, who might be able to help, except he's lost everything, including his son... Can a beautiful symphony of the heart come from such chaos?

All 6 Titles in the Queen of the Rockies Series:

Available in e-book, paperback, large print.

Queen of the Rockies (Sep. 2021)

Song of the Rockies (Oct. 2021)

Heart of the Rockies (Nov. 2021)

Flower of the Rockies (Dec. 2021)

Bride of the Rockies (Jan. 2021)

and *Flame of the Rockies (Feb. 2021)*

All part of this ongoing story of how Montana established herself through her women and the men that they loved.

Historical Novella from Angela with Barbour Publishing: *The Mail-Order Standoff* featuring Angela's story, *Right On Time,* set in 1883 Montana and Kentucky as the world changes, for a moment though, time stands still...

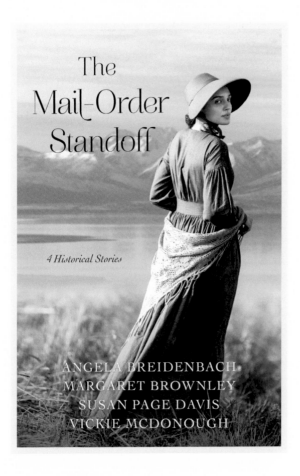

Nonfiction:

Awarded the Dove Faith-friendly Seal of Approval!

In paperback, e-book ... **And coming Fall 2021 Large Print**

Our experiences can be amazing opportunities to help others. But only if we learn to mine them for the gems of wisdom we've learned. Gems of Wisdom: The Treasure of Experience is about overcoming, gaining confidence and courage, and becoming a woman who embraces the destiny God built into our D.N.A. It's about becoming a woman of courage, confidence, and candor — and then using those gifts to help other women do the same.

Catch the special feature podcast, Grace Under Pressure, made just for this book. Episodes available on AngelaBreidenbach.com

This book is a work of fiction set in a real location. Any reference to historical figures, locations, or events, whether fictional or actual, is a fictional representation.

Biblical verses in this book of fiction are taken from Holy Bible, King James Version, KJV, Cambridge, 1769.

Scripture quotations marked (NLT) are taken from the Holy Bible, New Living Translation, copyright © 1996, 2004, 2007 by Tyndale House Foundation. Used by permission of Tyndale House Publishers, Inc., Carol Stream, Illinois 60188. All rights reserved.

Lyrics for *Away in the Manger* are public domain.

Cover Images and Cover Art Illustration by Period Images, Pi Creative Lab and Mary Chronis. Cover Text, Logo, and Branding by Angela Breidenbach.

Published in Missoula, Montana, by Gems Books, an imprint of Gems of Wisdom / Angela Eve Breidenbach LLC.

Library of Congress Cataloging-in-Publication Data

Breidenbach, Angela

Queen of the Rockies 2021 originally published as The Debutante Queen 2014, 2015, 2016.

Paperback—ISBN-13: 978-0-9980847-2-5

Fiction 2. Historical — Fiction 3. Romance — Fiction

E-book—ISBN-13: 978-0-998047-3-2

Fiction — Historical 2. Fiction — Romance — Western

Large Print—ISBN-13: 978-0-9980847-4-9

Fiction — Historical 2. Large Print